CRYSTAL

CRYSTAL

Helen Ashfield

ST. MARTIN'S PRESS
New York

Library of Congress Cataloging-in-Publication Data

Bennetts, Pamela.
    Crystal.

    "A Thomas Dunne Book."
    I. Title.
PR6052.E533C78   1987   823'.914   87-13134
ISBN 0-312-01028-1

First published in Great Britain by Robert Hale Limited.

First U.S. Edition
10 9 8 7 6 5 4 3 2 1

Acknowledgments

I am deeply indebted to the following authors whose works were not only fascinating to read but also provided me with the information I needed to write this novel:

Snuff: Yesterday and Today, C.W. Shepherd
Snuff and Snuff-Boxes, Hugh McCausland
Snuff Boxes, Kenneth Blakemore
Snuff Boxes – European & American, Clare le Corbeiller
Bristol in the 18C, Edited by Patrick McGrath
The City and County of Bristol, Bryan Little
Beau Brummell, Kathleen Campbell
Beau Brummell, Hubert Cole
Beau Brummell and His Times, Roger Boutet de Monvel
The Reign of Beau Brummell, Willard Connely
Beau Brummell: His Life and Letters, Lewis Melville
Handbook of English Costume in 19C, C. Willett Cunnington and Phillis Cunnington
The Fashionable Lady in the 19C, Charles H. Gibbs-Smith
Costume and Fashion 1760-1920, Jack Cassin-Scott

A special word of thanks to Fr Kenneth Loveless who gave me valuable information about snuff and snuff-boxes.

P.B.

CRYSTAL

One

London 1795

The day Martha Yorke met a violent death began much like any other.

Crystal, aged eight, was awake early. She rose from the damp floor, careful not to disturb the rest of her family with whom she shared the single room in a tall soot-laden house in Angel Court.

It wasn't really a court. It was just a bulge in one of the twisting alleys and side-streets which constituted the stews of St Giles. The houses weren't proper houses either. They were ruins which leaned crookedly against one another as if they dared not move so much as a brick lest the whole pack fell down.

Backyards were crammed with piles of rubbish and stolen goods hidden under sacks or whatever had come to hand. The courtyard itself oozed filth. Rotting vegetables, a dead cat or two, rags and paper mingled with the contents of chamber pots which were emptied from windows every morning.

Inside, the dwellings were no better. Every floor from attic to basement was packed to suffocating capacity with the dross of human life. Six or more to a room was usual. Most of the occupants were hungry, cold and dirty and quite a few of them diseased.

There were many slums in London, threaded amongst the tree-lined squares and gracious terraces where the rich lived, but most agreed that none had such a bad name as St Giles.

It was notorious for the number of criminals it sheltered. Its beggars, prostitutes, thieves, fences and escaped prisoners hidden there were dangerous, vicious, capable of anything.

There were old clothes shops in Monmouth Street where Samuel Yorke was sometimes able to unload his children's takings for the day. In Neal Street there were birds for sale, small, frantic creatures imprisoned in their cages. Further on there were shops and stalls selling cheap food for those who had a penny left after their visits to the local taverns. They stayed open seven days a week, none of the vendors recognizing God or the Sabbath which He had set aside for rest.

Crystal picked her way over the prostrate forms of her three brothers and went to the window. There was no question of washing, or tidying her matted hair. She had no comb and water was scarce, for the supply at the public pump was not turned on very often. What was left in the jug was wanted for drinking purposes, each drop precious.

Crystal rubbed clean a piece of cracked glass, gazing out at the cold October morning, shivering because her dress was so thin and torn. If there were ever any new clothes to be had they went to her sister, Rose. Rose was fourteen, proud of her looks, and her father's favourite. She had been on the game for a year and Yorke boasted of the fact as he pocketed the coins she handed over to him.

It was only when the others were asleep that Crystal felt free. They might snore or toss and turn, but they weren't arguing, jabbering or cursing at one another. In the merciful silence of dawn, Crystal's thoughts took wings as she considered her future.

No one looking at the scrawny child would guess she had such a fierce determination inside her. Her one aim was to get away from Angel Court as soon as she was old enough. Her resolve to better herself was implacable; she wouldn't let herself become a down-trodden wreck like her mother.

For a second Crystal turned to look at Martha. In sleep, there was still a hint of the prettiness which had once been hers. When she awoke she would revert to the tired, defeated woman whose body had sagged along with her hopes and spirit until she looked like a bundle of rags tied in the middle.

Sometimes, when they were alone, Crystal asked her mother why she had married Yorke.

''E weren't always like 'e is now,' Martha would say, sighing for a past long gone. ''E were strong and 'andsome and 'e treated me well at first.'

When taxed as to why Samuel had become a callous brute with a temper as taut as the string on a violin, Martha would just shrug.

'It were the drink,' she would reply. 'It's addled 'is brain, I reckon.'

Crystal went to the tiny grate filled with odd pieces of wood, a worn tinder-box on the hearth. She managed to get the fire going, tipping water into a blackened cauldron to heat it up. Usually, water was all there was to be had, but two days ago Jamie Yorke had exchanged a packet of tea for a silver watch he had purloined. He knew his mother would have no use for a time-piece, but he had felt a warm glow as he watched her pleasure as she sipped her hot tea. It was a luxury and each brown leaf was treasured as if it had been a diamond.

Although Crystal grew impatient with her mother from time to time, because the latter wouldn't stand up to her husband, she loved her dearly and did whatever she could to help her. She was cutting up a stale loaf, meticulously measuring each slice so that all would get fair shares, when Yorke stirred. After that there was the usual pandemonium.

Samuel kicked Jamie, Danny and Eli until they were on their feet, then turned to the younger girls, pulling them up by their hair until they screeched in pain.

Martha was groggy that morning, sick to her stomach. She knew there was another child on the way but hadn't had the courage to tell Samuel. Another mouth to feed, however sparingly, would be that much less for him to spend on gin.

Finally, everyone gathered round the unsteady table, the boys sitting on boxes, Martha on a stool, only Samuel favoured with what had once been a chair. The girls had to stand, Ivy's head only just visible as she drank greedily from her chipped mug.

Then Yorke gave his flock their orders, directing Jamie and Danny to Covent Garden and Eli to Oxford Street, because he was the most dextrous at picking pockets. Ivy, aged four, was to be hired out for the day to a professional beggar. Her sad blue eyes and rosebud mouth normally aroused generosity in those who saw her wretchedness and she was much sought-after by the drabs who whined on street corners for their living.

'And you two,' he said, turning to Crystal and Aggie, who was rising seven. 'See what you can get from the market in Holborn. Keep your eyes and wits about yer and don't come back empty-'anded unless you want trouble.'

'What about me, pa?'

Samuel looked at Rose who was regarding him slyly from under curling lashes. His voice softened slightly as he gave her the nearest thing he ever got to a smile.

'You'll go to Drury Lane, same as always.'

'Oh, pa! There are too many like me there already. Let me work Regent Street, just for once.'

He glowered.

'I said Drury Lane and Drury Lane I meant. Less of your lip, my girl, or I'll take the skin off your back.'

'You won't.' Rose was very sure of herself as she returned her father's smile. 'How can I please a man if I can't lie down?'

There was a moment's silence, every eye on Yorke, waiting to see how he would take Rose's impudence. his thick eyebrows were beginning to knit, his porcine eyes filling with anger. When he gave a sudden rusty chuckle, the sighs of relief wafted round the table like a summer's breeze.

'Go on, then,' he said, rising to his full six-foot height, stretching brawny arms above his head. 'Git goin', but if you don't find no customers there, it'll be the worse for you.'

After that they all went their separate ways, Samuel stomping off to Rat's Castle, his favourite tavern. Martha did her best to clean up before she left to scrub floors at one of the nearby brothels, but the place looked no better in spite of her efforts. It was all so hopeless and she felt more queasy than ever. There was a woman she'd heard of in Milk Alley, but that took money. Maybe if she worked a few extra hours something could be done before Samuel realised she was pregnant again. It was worth a try. Anything was better than one of Yorke's beatings.

Crystal was the first one home that evening. Aggie had met Rose and was waiting for her sister as she gossiped with friends on the corner. Crystal had never stolen a thing in her life and, but for Jamie who always gave her something from his own haul, she would have fared badly at her father's hands.

She was grateful to Jamie for his generosity and kindness.

Part of her plans for the future involved the salvation of her eldest brother, his removal from St Giles, and the purchase for him of a business of his own. It never occurred to Crystal that Jamie was quite happy as he was. He found thieving a challenge and had recently struck up a friendship with an ageing madam two streets away. She was hot for his strong young body and paid him in food, drink, and money, which his father knew nothing about. If he had realised that his sister wanted him to do an honest day's work he would have been appalled.

As Crystal reached the door of the fifth floor back she was aware that her father's shouting was louder than usual and that the single, piercing scream from her mother was something she had never heard before.

When she saw Martha on the floor, her head and face covered in blood, Crystal nearly fainted, holding on to the door-knob for support. Samuel still had the poker in his hand, its tip stained an ominous red. At last Crystal managed to get a whisper through her parched lips.

'You've killed her. You've killed ma!'

As Yorke blundered drunkenly towards her he tried to bluff it out.

'No I ain't. She's only knocked out.'

'She's dead!' Crystal knew it without a doubt. The body was too still, the wounds too terrible for there to be any life left in Martha Yorke. 'You've murdered her.'

Then she turned and began to run down the rickety stairs, hearing her father thundering after her. Outside, the cobblestones were slippery for it had been raining for some time. It didn't stop Crystal's headlong flight. She knew that once Yorke caught her she, too, would die, and terror urged her on like a spur as she disappeared into the labyrinth beyond Angel Court.

She had no idea how far she had run when she paused to

get her breath. It seemed to her to be miles and miles, but her father might have moved just as fast. She waited, breath held in, but there were no footsteps to be heard and she could afford to slow down to a walk as she put further distance between herself and the deadly poker.

Two hours later, after many stops, she knew she was finished. She was weak with hunger, shock, and exertion and had to take cover until the morning. She didn't know where she was, but there were smart carriages passing in the street, their cheerful candles alight in glass holders, liveried footmen up behind. As they went by, they illuminated briefly the shops outside which Crystal had come to a halt. She could see that they were elegant places, with bow-windows, their painted boards spick and span, the brass knockers on their closed doors gleaming like gold. They also had front areas which one could reach by a spiral iron staircase. Cautiously, Crystal opened the gate of one which had been left ajar, creeping down as quiet as a mouse. Unlike the gate, the doors to the house and those which housed coal and wood were tightly shut. All that was left was a corner where rain pattered down, forming a pool. The wetness didn't matter to Crystal; she was soaked already. All she cared about was the denseness of the shadows.

She made herself as small as possible, hugging her knees to her chin, hearing her heart thudding loudly. She shut her eyes as she tried to blot out the awful picture of her mother. She would never see her again, nor her brothers and sisters, come to that. She could never go home to where her father was waiting for her.

Before the real seriousness of her predicament could penetrate her dazed mind she began to nod. The rain grew heavier, a wind driving it into her like sharp arrows, but she didn't notice.

Crystal Yorke, late of Angel Court, had fallen asleep.

Basil Corry was humming to himself as he shaved. He was a neat, fastidious man, always well dressed, but never trying to out-vie his customers. That would have been unwise; the *haut monde* liked those who served them to keep their places.

Four years had passed since he had become the proud owner of the shop in exclusive Swan Street, just off St James's. His satisfaction was still mixed with surprise at the turn his life had taken. The son of a respectable manufacturer, he had been apprenticed to a goldsmith who made snuff-boxes for those with a great deal of money to spend. Basil enjoyed the work, nimble of fingers and quick to pick up the intricacies of his trade. He had expected to spend the rest of his days as a mere assistant, but Fortune had chosen him as one of its darlings.

His French godmother had seen the Revolution in France coming long before the storming of the Bastille. She had packed up her goods and chattels, including her fabulous collection of snuff-boxes, and repaired to England where she lived for the last three years of her life. She had demanded that Basil visit her and had taken a liking to him. His enthusiasm for his work amused her; his scrupulous politeness won her approval.

When she died, Corry found himself not only possessed of a nice little nest-egg, but also the five hundred and fifty exquisite boxes which she had acquired over a long period. By this time, Corry's father was also dead and not hovering about to warn his son of the folly of taking the gamble which he had in mind.

When Basil came across the empty shop in Swan Street he had seen it as a sign from heaven and promptly purchased it. He refurbished the interior, painted the outside, took on an assistant expert in chasing, a cook-housekeeper, and a maid to do the cleaning.

It didn't take long for society to discover Corry's treasure house. They cried in disbelief at his boxes, each a work of art in gold, gems, enamel and silver. He demanded high prices and got them, whilst Benjamin Brooker worked away in a cramped room at the back of the shop producing more gold and silver trifles. Some were sold as they were; others were sent to specialists in painting enamel *en plein*, or to jewellers who added rubies, emeralds, sapphires and diamonds to enhance their worth.

Corry was utterly content with his existence. He felt no desire to take a wife, for she might upset the smooth running of his business. Once or twice he had sought the company of the ladies of the night, but decided that sexual antics were an overrated pastime and buried himself in his work.

When he heard the sharp knock on his bedroom door he frowned. Fanny Bethall, his maid, had already brought up his cup of hot chocolate which he sipped whilst he dressed. No one ever disturbed him after that until he made his way to the dining-room to partake of breakfast.

He had a premonition that the tranquillity of his routine was about to be shattered and when he gave a reluctant order to enter, he was sure of it.

Mrs Moloney was the ideal housekeeper; buxom, scrupulously clean, civil, and even-tempered. She coped with Corry's ménage with smooth efficiency, never ruffled even if the butcher did deliver mutton chops instead of best beef, or the milk arrived twenty minutes late.

But that morning her calm was thinly-layered over agitation and Corry's heart sank. He hoped she wasn't about to give notice, for he knew he would never find another woman as suitable as Winnie Moloney. Then his mind darted to his stock which he had hidden away in a back store as usual. Was it possible that a thief had entered during the night, despite his precautions? He blanched at the prospect of such a disaster, but Mrs Moloney soon put that idea out of his head.

When she had finished telling her tale, almost incoherent, he said faintly:

'I don't understand. You say you found a child in the area?'

'That we did, sir; leastways, Fanny found her. Soaked right through, the poor mite, and goodness knows when she last had a proper meal.'

The thought of a wet and starving child taking refuge on his premises was almost as bad as losing a housekeeper or his stock. Basil had never had anything to do with the young, being an only child, and his first instinct was to tell Winnie to get rid of her.

His heart sank further still at the intelligence that his unwelcome guest was already in the house and that Fanny was plying her with porridge to line her ribs.

'Well,' he said at last. 'I'll come and see her, but of course she can't stay here. It's quite out of the question. This is a shop, not an orphanage.'

He followed his housekeeper to the kitchen, as spotless as Mrs Moloney herself. His first sight of Crystal confirmed his worst fears. She was the dirtiest human being he had ever seen. Her hair and skin were covered with grime and he was certain that she was host to a whole army of lice.

He listened to Crystal's story in silence. Crystal knew that she dared not tell anyone about her murdered mother because the officers of the law would be called at once to deal with Samuel Yorke. That would mean her brothers and sisters would be taken to the workhouse and even Angel Court was better than that. She hated lying to the man who was gazing at her in consternation, but there was nothing else for it.

' … so when me ma died, too,' she finished, 'I had to get out of the room we had, 'cos I'd got no money. I've been looking for work since then, but no one seems to want me.'

That at least was true and Crystal clenched her fists in her lap, waiting for Mr Corry to throw her out neck and crop. Fanny had told her the jeweller's name and the fact that she had been hiding in a very select district in the West End of London. Corry wouldn't want anyone like her spoiling the splendour of his home. Crystal hadn't got further than the kitchen, but that was enough to tell her how rich he must be. She had never seen such a place and in between mouthfuls of fresh bread and butter had admired every last polished copper pot and each piece of sparkling china set out on the dresser. Even the black stove seemed to shine and its warmth was like something from a dream.

'How long have you been wandering about?'

Crystal flushed, adding another lie.

'A week or two.'

'Good gracious me.' Basil was at a loss. His proper course was clear enough to him and he had stated it firmly to Mrs Moloney. But somehow it was hard to find the right words to put the waif on the streets again. 'Well, you'd better have a bath, I suppose. Then we'll see what's to be done with you.'

Crystal had no experience of baths and as the rosy-cheeked Fanny came in with a large tin receptacle and began to fill it with hot water she was somewhat alarmed. But when the soap was rubbed all over her by Mrs Moloney's strong fingers, Crystal started to enjoy the sensation. She squeaked a bit as the knots in her hair were unravelled, but the towels which dried her smelt of lavender and she sighed in pleasure.

Mrs Moloney and Fanny stared at their finished work in

amazement, but when Crystal had been clothed in one of Fanny's dresses, several sizes too large for her, Basil Corry was even more stunned.

He thought he had never encountered such beauty in a girl in all his life. The hair, which he had imagined to be dark, was a bright, shining red. The skin, now relieved of its coating of dust, was like cream. The small nose and perfect mouth helped to achieve the loveliness before him, but it was the eyes which reduced him to temporary silence. They were green, like emeralds, large, clear and utterly bewitching. Finally, he said blankly:

'You've got red hair. Well I never.'

He saw the blush on Crystal's cheeks and knew then that he wouldn't be able to turn her out. He glanced at Mrs Moloney and Fanny, both full of trepidation.

'What shall we do, sir?' asked Winnie as Corry made no move. 'Give 'er a bit of summat and let 'er go?'

Crystal and the other two women waited for sentence to be passed and it seemed to them ages before the master of the house made his pronouncement.

'Go?' Basil pulled himself together, knowing he was about to do something extremely foolish. 'Where can she go to? No, you'd better go and buy her something to wear, Mrs Moloney. She'll have to share your room, Fanny; there's nowhere else to put her.'

As Mrs Moloney's and Fanny's faces lit up, Crystal got to her feet.

'Do you really mean it? I wouldn't want to stay in a place as wonderful as this if I were turned out in a day or two's time. It would be worse than going now, wouldn't it?'

Corry was irritated by the lump which had risen in his throat, transfixed by the brilliant eyes in which so much heartbreak could be read.

'Yes it would, and I do mean that you can stay. You can work here in the living-quarters and when you're older you can help Benjamin in the workroom. Heaven knows he's untidy enough to need someone to clear up after him.'

Fanny, an ash-blonde with blue eyes and a kind heart, went to put her arms round Crystal.

'There, didn't I say it would be all right?'

'Yes, but I wasn't sure.' Crystal was trembling as she turned back to Corry. 'I won't be a nuisance, I promise. I'll do all that you and Mrs Moloney tell me to, and I won't eat much.'

Mrs Moloney blew her nose furtively and Basil cleared his throat, still trying to get rid of the vexatious lump.

'You must eat as much as you want,' he said firmly. 'You need fattening up, anyone can see that. I don't know why you chose my shop to shelter in last night, but these things always have a reason.'

'I'm truly grateful, sir.' Crystal couldn't quite believe what was happening, afraid that the bubble of happiness might burst in her hand. 'I really do thank you.'

Basil nodded and went off to set out the snuff-boxes on their lush velvet beds. That morning the jewels in them didn't look so bright and he knew why. They were cold, dead stones, but Crystal Yorke was gloriously alive and far more beautiful than any of his wares.

He stood back to consider his arrangement of a group of *en cage* boxes with Sèvres porcelain panels and shook his head.

'Corry, you're an idiot,' he said aloud, and then went upstairs again to where his breakfast awaited him.

At the same time as Crystal was being rescued by Corry and his staff, a house party was in progress at Levenden Hall, one of the country seats of Graham Haversham, Marquis of Ravenmore.

The house was a sprawl of old red bricks set against a rising bank of trees and surrounded by green lawns, flower beds, orchards and summer houses.

The marquis was tall, elegant and reserved, with light brown eyes, thin lips, and the Haversham nose, high bridged and arrogant. The servants had just placed in front of the marchioness a large silver lamp tea urn, flanked by cups, saucers and plates of finest eggshell china. The silverware was heavy and expensive, the delicacies a temptation to any palate.

Ravenmore would rather have been at the stables discussing with his head groom the new stallion he had just acquired. As there was no hope of such freedom for a while he surveyed those present, assessing them carefully so that none should know they were being watched.

First, he looked at his wife, Hildegarde, a small woman with pansy-brown eyes and an unhappy droop to her mouth. Theirs had been an arranged marriage which had worked well enough, but Graham had never loved Hildegarde and occasionally felt guilty because of it.

Next to her were two elderly cousins of his, Louise and Laetitia Josslyn. They kept to their rooms as much as possible because, as they said to each other as they scuttled to their sanctuaries, modern children were allowed far too much licence. It was the age of practical jokes and one could never be quite sure what the three youngsters in the party might be getting up to. Louise and Laetitia looked as poor as church mice in their quiet, almost drab, garb. In fact, both were ridiculously rich and doted on Stuart, Earl of Melfort, the marquis's son and heir, to whom they intended to bequeath their wealth.

Marcus and Daphne Somerset, Earl and Countess of Selkirk, were the next subjects of the marquis's scrutiny. Marcus was short and thick-set; very good natured, with an underlying strength of character which others didn't always notice. Daphne was dark-haired with violet eyes and a saucy, inviting smile.

Their children, Rupert, Viscount Dunstone, and Lady Charlotte, were arguing about something, careful to keep their voices low so that they did not incur parental displeasure. It had been taken for granted that Charlotte would marry Stuart in the fulness of time. The marquis wasn't quite certain how the notion had started, but he had no objection. The girl's pedigree was sound, she was as pretty and vivacious as her mother, and he sensed an inner goodness below the mischievous surface.

Ravenmore had no such charitable thoughts towards her brother. He had never liked Rupert although he wasn't sure why that was so. The boy was comely enough and almost excessively polite, but the marquis always felt a sense of disquiet when the viscount was present.

Finally, he looked at Stuart and was rather pleased with himself. His son was tall, strong and graceful, typically Haversham in looks, although he was too young for life to have made the well-shaped mouth hard. He had hazel eyes and a skin which responded easily to the sun. A handsome creature of fifteen; six months older than Rupert, two years older than Charlotte.

At last the ritual of tea-time was over. The cousins vanished as if by magic, the marquis made for the stables and Marcus took a nap while Daphne and Hildegarde gossiped.

Stuart and Charlotte returned to the orchard to the north of the house. It was one of their favourite places and both were quite glad that Rupert hadn't accompanied them.

'I hope you'll sleep well tonight, Melfort,' said Charlotte with a wicked demureness which Stuart knew of old. 'I like to think of you comfortably bedded.'

Stuart laughed.

'I don't think you really meant that last bit but, as to the soundness of my sleep, have no fear. I have already removed the toad you so unkindly placed between my sheets.'

'A pox on you!' Charlotte was vexed for a moment. 'Why do you always know when I'm playing a trick on you?'

'Because you give yourself away. You'll never make a card player unless you can control that smug look of yours.'

'Well – ' She was resigned. 'I daresay the toad would have expired before nightfall anyway. Rupert's put some spiders in Cousin Laetitia's bed.'

The earl raised his eyebrows.

'Has he indeed? Then we'd better go and take them out again, hadn't we?'

'But why? Laetitia will have a fit when she finds them and it will be the most tremendous laugh.'

'Not if the fit is a real one. It's time you learned on whom you can play such pranks and those you must leave in peace. You're thirteen, Charlie, not five.'

For a moment Charlotte looked mutinous, but the earl's outstretched hand couldn't be ignored, neither could the look in his eyes.

'All right, but you're a spoilsport.'

'Perhaps.'

'And you're not a bit like Rupert.'

'I'm glad to hear it.'

'Stuart! He's my brother and he'll dare anything. He told me this morning that he went down to the servants' hall and cut a lock of hair from one of the kitchenmaids. It seems that she had hysterics and an old servant who saw him gave him a real tongue-lashing, but Rupert didn't care.'

'Is there anything he does care about, except himself?'

Charlotte didn't have time to defend her brother again because they had reached the upper floor where a fine to-do was going on. Daphne Somerset was in tears, the marchioness trying to comfort her. Marcus, never at his best when there was a crisis involving women, was shifting from one foot to the other, looking round as if seeking a bolt-hole.

Louise and Laetitia had crept out of their rooms, agog. This was the sort of excitement they could relish because they were not called upon to take any part in it. They could merely enjoy the unexpected break in the monotony of their lives.

Stuart thought perhaps the toad intended for him had found its way into the countess's bed, but when he looked at his father's grim face he realised that something was seriously wrong.

'What is it?' he asked above Daphne's wails. 'Is someone ill?'

'No.' The marquis was bleak. 'The countess has lost a valuable ring. She saw it before she went down to the drawing-room for tea. Now it's gone.'

'But it can't have.' Stuart rejected the idea out of hand. 'Lady Daphne, are you sure you've looked in the right place?'

'Yes she has, dear.' The marchioness was close to tears herself, for such a thing had never happened in her house before. 'We've all looked – everywhere.'

'Perhaps I can help, although I don't like to – well – it's rather embarrassing.'

Everyone turned to look at Rupert who seemed to have appeared from nowhere. Ravenmore raised his quizzing-glass and ran a frosty eye over Dunstone.

'What is embarrassing? If you know something about this affair, Rupert, for pity's sake let us hear it.'

Rupert's face was a study in virtue.

'Well, my lord, it's just that when I came up here a while ago to fetch something, I saw one of the maids going into mother's room. She kept looking over her shoulder as if she were nervous. I thought it odd and almost asked her what she was doing but, of course, I didn't. It is not my place to question your servants.'

'Indeed it isn't.' The marquis was frowning. 'Would you recognise the maid if you saw her again? One looks very much like another to me.'

'Oh yes, I'd know her. She had grey hair and she limped.'

'Latterman!' Hildegarde caught her breath. 'No, she wouldn't, I'm sure she wouldn't. She's worked here for so many years. I think you must be mistaken, Rupert.'

'I'm sure I wasn't. Have you any other crippled servants?'

'Hildegarde,' said the marquis shortly, 'send for Latterman and let's see what she's got to say. We must get to the bottom of this.'

Stuart hadn't taken his eyes off Rupert since the latter had first begun his tale. An old servant had, in Charlotte's words, given him a tongue-lashing for a spiteful act. Latterman was old, but surely even Dunstone wouldn't – At that moment the viscount turned his head and looked at Stuart and the last doubt in the earl's mind faded.

When Latterman arrived she was as white as a ghost, her hands trembling when the questions were put to her. Her denials were vehement, her sobs smothering her protests.

But there was no help for it. The maid's room had to be searched to placate the countess, and to assure her that her host and hostess did not think her son a liar.

The ring was found, as Stuart knew it would be, tucked amongst Latterman's pathetic, well darned underwear.

The maid screamed of her innocence, but Hildegarde had no choice but to dismiss her summarily and without a reference.

While his mother was making humble apologies to the countess for the disgraceful behaviour of one of her staff, the earl looked at his father, opening his mouth to demand more proof. The marquis quelled the words before they could be uttered, and Stuart ground his teeth silently.

It would be difficult to prove that Rupert was guilty and it was obvious that the marquis was not going to let him try. The Haversham hospitality had been violated, their honour dented by one of their retainers, and that was an end of it.

But as the small crowd dispersed and Stuart passed close to his father the latter said softly:

'I will deal with it; don't interfere.'

The earl was startled.

'You mean, my lord, you think that Rupert – '

'I never think about Rupert Somerset unless I have to. Nothing can be done about that, but Latterman will be well cared for.'

Then Ravenmore walked away and the earl went slowly downstairs to join Charlotte.

'You're angry, aren't you?' she said as they made their way to a folly containing a love-seat carved in stone. 'I can see it.'

'I'm not angry with you.'

'I know that. I mean about your mother's maid. It is hard, I realise that, but she had to be punished.'

'If she were guilty.'

Charlotte stared at the taut line of Stuart's mouth.

'But of course she was guilty. Mother's ring was found in her room.'

'It doesn't follow that she put it there. I didn't put a toad in my bed.'

'Stuart! What are you saying?' The colour had drained from Charlotte's cheeks. 'You don't think that I – ?'

'Of course not.' He gave her a quick smile. 'Credit me with some intelligence, Charlie.'

'Then who? You mean that perhaps one of the other maids had a grudge against Latterman and hid the ring in her drawer to get her into trouble?'

'I did not say that.'

'But what else is left? Who else could have put it there?'

The earl almost spoke, but his father's order was clear, concise and not to be disobeyed.

'I don't suppose we'll ever know, but we've talked about your mother's ring enough for one day. Come on: I'll teach you to play faro and keep your face straight at the same time. Don't worry, Charlie; it's all over. There's nothing you and I can do about it now.'

Two

The next two weeks in Crystal's life passed like a dream. Mrs Moloney took her to the market where she and Fanny bought their clothes. Crystal was overcome by the worsted petticoats, linen dresses, white aprons and muslin kerchiefs to wear round her shoulders. There were stockings and shoes of Spanish leather, red bedgowns and a brown twill mantle set off by a chip-straw hat with a green ribbon round the crown.

'So much,' she said in the faint voice. 'You've bought three of almost everything. It will cost a fortune.'

Mrs Moloney had a chuckle like rich brown chocolate.

'Master's orders, luv. Can't work for a man like 'im and not be decently turned out. 'Sides, 'e said 'e wanted you to look nice.'

Crystal had suffered many hardships in her short life and withstood the blows without crying. Mr Corry's kindness brought tears to her eyes which Winnie pretended not to notice.

The room which Crystal shared with Fanny was another source of wonderment to her. There was a faded but serviceable carpet on the floor, pretty curtains at the window, plump pallets, and plenty of blankets. There were hooks behind the door for outer garments; chests for clothes not in use. It was warm and dry and Crystal thought it

must be the most luxurious place in the world until she
began to help Fanny clean her employer's well appointed
home.

The furniture had simple, graceful lines, always shining
as a result of Fanny's elbow-grease. Carpets were thick,
drapes at the tall windows were made of heavy brocade.
Crystal was terrified to touch the valuable china
ornaments, leaving those to her friend whilst she rubbed
away at brass fenders and blackened grates.

At the beginning of the third week Crystal knew she
couldn't maintain the lie she had told Basil Corry. He had
been too good to her and he deserved the truth. So did Mrs
Moloney and Fanny, come to that, and she explained the
situation to them first, her cheeks hot with shame. She
expected them to back away from a liar and the daughter of
a murderer, but they didn't.

'You poor little beggar,' said Winnie, sniffing a bit. 'A
proper time you've 'ad of it, 'aven't you?'

'I ought to have told you about my father at once.'

'Maybe, but it's easy to see why you didn't.' Fanny was
quick to reassure the child whom she already looked upon
as a sister. 'Don't knows that I'd 'ave done any different
from you.'

'Still you're right to want to put things straight with the
master.' Mrs Moloney put her handkerchief away. 'He's
in the library with all them dratted books we 'ave to dust.
Why don't you go and git it over, eh?'

Basil listened to Crystal in silence, shocked at the
thought of what the small girl in front of him must have felt
when she saw the body of her mother covered in blood.

'And I'm truly sorry I fibbed,' said Crystal, looking
down at the floor. 'I'll never lie to you again, that is, if
you'll let me stay after what I've done.'

Basil sighed. He wasn't used to dealing with domestic

dramas of such gigantic proportions. Indeed, he wasn't used to coping with dramas of any kind, but he recognised that having taken Crystal into his home he had accepted responsibility for her.

'Of course you may stay,' he said gently. 'What a terrible experience it must have been for you. Did you love your mother very much?'

Crystal raised her head.

'Yes – '

'But – ?'

'She didn't fight, sir. I wouldn't have let my father, or any man, treat me like that.'

The faintest smile touched Corry's lips.

'Yes, you're a fighter, aren't you? A survivor, one might say. Well, I suppose we'd better find out what's happened to your father and the rest of the family.'

Crystal was horrified.

'Sir, you can't go to Angel Court! It's an awful place and the people there are all bad. They'd attack and rob you.'

'Don't worry, I shan't go myself. I know a man who can make enquiries for us and even the blackest villain in St Giles won't take him on. I'll let you know when I have some news.'

When Corry sent for Crystal again she found that her heart was beating rapidly, the palms of her hands damp. The last few days had been nervous ones, waiting to know the fate of Jamie, Danny, Eli and the girls.

Corry was compassionate as he saw Crystal's face.

'My dear, there is really no easy way to tell you what my agent has discovered.'

Crystal's chin went up.

'I know that, sir. I won't grizzle or have the vapours, I promise. Just tell me what's happened.'

She listened to Corry, feeling a trifle sick. Samuel Yorke

had been arrested and would almost certainly hang. All three boys had vanished on the night their mother died. Aggie and Ivy were in the workhouse. Rose was still plying her trade as if nothing had happened.

'Try to put it all behind you.' Corry was worried by Crystal's unnatural calm. She had kept her vow; no tear, no vapours. But he saw the look in her eyes and grieved for her. 'You can do nothing to change things and neither can anyone else. Your life is here now. Mrs Moloney, Fanny and I will make it as happy for you as we can.'

Basil was as good as his word. Gradually, as the past faded, Crystal blossomed in the hot-house of affection in Swan Street. She worked alongside Fanny, scrubbing, polishing, cleaning, her bones no longer sticking through her skin, her smile a measure of her contentment.

Now and then, as a treat, she was allowed to go downstairs to the shop after it had closed. As Basil took each precious bauble from its setting to put it away for the night, he would tell Crystal something about it.

'Now this,' he said one evening, amused by Crystal's awed expression, 'is a copy of one originally made by a man called Noël Hardivilliers. See the musicians on the lid? They're Chinese.'

'And that one?'

Corry glanced at Crystal in her neat frock and apron, the candlelight making a blazing halo of her curls. Her face no longer looked haunted; her beauty still took his breath away. She should have worn silks and satins when she grew up, but he doubted if she ever would.

'Chased gold and lapis-lazuli,' he said, dismissing his daydreaming. 'My godmother told me it was made by Juste-Aurèle Meissonnier of Paris, but I'm sure she was wrong. Louis XV of France had one exactly the same and I don't think it's likely that the king would have allowed a second to be made. Still, someone made it and it's a handsome piece, isn't it?'

'It's beautiful.' Crystal watched in reverence as it was carefully wrapped up. 'What about that one? The one with painted lid and sides?'

'Ah yes, a nice piece. *Basse-taille* enamelling. See how the artist has cut out small sections of the gold and filled them with translucent enamel of different thicknesses.'

As the months passed, Crystal learned from Corry all about the boxes from the time when they were just thin sheets of metal until the last tiny pearl or diamond had been put into place.

He told her about the master goldsmiths of Paris who, before the French Revolution, had their workshops on the Quai des Orfèvres and around the Place Dauphine on the Ile de la Cité.

She was shewn examples of such masters as Gouers, Moser and Bergs, famous for their gold-chased boxes, and George, Ducrollay and de Mailly, who specialised in enamelling. She was told all about machine engraving on a *tour à guillocher*, or rose engine, and listened entranced to tales of others who worked as gravers, chasers, and experts in chinoiserie, who added slivers of tinted shell to sheets of mother-of-pearl; the lapidaries who polished small panels of agate, and the glyptic workers who were skilled in the engraving of stones.

When she was twelve, Crystal was allowed to help Benjamin Booker in the cramped and stuffy workroom behind the shop. Booker was a dour man and wasn't at all sure that he wanted a slip of a girl fidgeting round him while he was working. Crystal sensed his initial animosity and crept about like a wraith. She soon learned to keep his tools clean and placed in exactly the right position. Benjamin said nothing, but he had stopped scowling. Now and then he would glance up at the wide-eyed child when she drew nearer to watch his artistry, secretly pleased by her admiration.

He used a tiny chisel struck by a hammer to push the gold or silver metal aside, forming a furrow on the lid or sides of the boxes. Then he would tap again, the furrow growing longer with each succeeding blow. It was delicate work and one false move could ruin a day's work. Feathers, coats of arms, flowers, intricate patterns of all kinds sprang from under Booker's skilful fingers and Crystal would sigh with deep satisfaction every time a box was completed.

Corry hadn't made the mistake of using up all his godmother's boxes at once. He made many journeys to Holland, Germany and other places in Europe to buy best quality merchandise to eke out his own treasures and the boxes made by Benjamin. Those who patronised his shop never knew when a few genuine Paris boxes would appear and so they kept coming back, hoping to steal a march on other eager collectors.

The years had wrought remarkable changes in Crystal. Basil had not only filled her stomach with food; he had nourished her mind as well. He found a respectable Dame School to which Crystal had been packed off for three hours a day. It wasn't long before she had outstripped the Dame in her knowledge, but Basil was something of a scholar and he found he enjoyed tutoring his young assistant. She was so quick to drink in every snippet of information and her enthusiasm was infectious. Sometimes Corry wondered if she wasn't trying too hard, but he never checked her. As he himself had said, she was a survivor and survivors needed a good education.

On her sixteenth birthday Crystal was cleaning out a store and discovered a large crate which was to change her life yet again.

'What is bankruptcy stock?' she asked that night as she and Basil went through the usual ritual of putting the snuff-boxes away. 'What does it mean?'

'Bankruptcy stock? Why do you ask?'

'Well, there's a big packing case in the store near the back door. I hadn't seen the writing on it until today, but that's what it said.'

'Shew me. I don't remember such a case.'

Together they made their way to the store, candles in hand, groping about until they found what they wanted. Basil opened the crate and let out an exclamation.

'Heavens! I'd forgotten all about these. They must have been here for years. There was a man called Scott who lost every penny in a bad business venture. He owed me money and as he couldn't pay in coin he gave me these instead.'

'But what are they?'

'Snuff-boxes.'

Crystal gasped in dismay as Basil placed one of them in the palm of her hand.

'Gold boxes? Kept like this?'

Corry smiled.

'Christopher Pinchbeck would have been flattered if he could have heard you. These aren't gold, but an alloy. Of course, people had been trying to find a cheap substitute for gold for centuries, without success. Then Pinchbeck, a watchmaker, found that by mixing eighty-three parts of pure rose copper and seventeen parts of pure zinc, which he got from China, he could produce a metal that was very similar to twenty-two-carat gold. Clever man. He made automata, too. A friend of my grandfather's – that's how I know just how Christopher did the trick.'

'They do look like gold and is that really enamel?'

'Yes, but not decorated, as you see.'

'Could anyone paint them?' In the half-light Crystal's

eyes gleamed. 'Mr Corry, do you think I could paint them?'

'You could try. Now I recall it, there were paints and other stuff sent to me with this lot. Yes, you could decorate a few. Benjamin will have to get the furnace in the yard going.'

'Why? Do they have to be heated? Won't they melt?'

'No, one has a muffle oven to prevent that. When one hand-paints boxes they have to be fired after a few strokes of the brush. That fixes the colour. Then you start again to deepen the hue and fire once more. It'll take a lot of patience.'

'I've got a lot to spare.'

'Yes, I think you have. Let me see, it's your birthday today, isn't it?'

She laughed.

'You know it is. You have given me that lovely tortoise-shell brush, comb and mirror.'

'And now I'm giving you the unfortunate Mr Scott's bankruptcy stock. You've seen what the great masters did. Now you try your hand.'

In the following year, Crystal produced a number of charming samples. She had plenty of failures at first, but she wasn't put off by them. Basil Corry had put a trade into her hands and she meant to make good use of his gift. Benjamin shewed her how to use the furnace and muffle oven and offered her odd bits of advice now and then. When she had produced two dozen flawless specimens, Basil found an outlet for her work.

The middle-classes were growing more affluent and were demanding some of the luxuries enjoyed by their superiors. However, even the most successful business man couldn't aspire to Corry's prices. Thus, when a friend of Basil's, who lived in Holborn, put a few of Crystal's pieces in his window amongst the china and glass ornaments they sold like hot cakes.

On her eighteenth birthday Crystal finished her fiftieth box, presenting it to Mrs Moloney with a shy kiss. Crystal had insisted that Basil should take most of the proceeds of the sale of her goods. The materials were really his, she had said firmly, and she wanted to repay at least part of his kindness to her. Corry knew it was useless to argue with Crystal when her mind was made up, but he put the money away safely for a day when his protégée might need it.

Sometimes, when she was sweeping up after Benjamin, Crystal would peep through a knot-hole in the wood, watching Basil's fashionable customers debating amongst themselves which box to purchase.

The morning after her birthday she saw a man enter the shop, struck at once by the quiet elegance of his attire and air of supreme confidence. It seemed to her that Corry's bow was lower than usual, his voice hushed with respect. It was a very long time before the young man made up his mind, selecting a box of gold, decorated with niello work. Crystal knew that it had come from Basil's special stock and it was obvious that the customer had a keen eye for the real thing.

'Who was that?' she asked, when Corry went into the workshop to have a word with Benjamin. 'He seemed to be a very important person. Is he royalty?'

Corry gave a wry smile.

'Worse than that; much worse. That was George Bryan Brummell, and it behoves us all to keep on the right side of him. One word from the Beau and a shopkeeper could be ruined. Where Brummell goes, society follows. When he avoids a place, the whole world shuns it. He's the most influential man of the day. Even the Prince of Wales bows to his judgment.'

'How odd.' Crystal was puzzled. 'You mean his status is higher than the Prince's?'

'In some ways. I'll tell you about Brummell when I've got the time, although I'm not sure I really understand myself how he got where he is.

'I don't suppose you'll ever meet him but, if you do, remember this. Insult whom you will, including kings and princes, but don't upset Brummell. If he should frown on you nothing could save you, not even your pretty face.'

'I'm glad I shan't meet him.' Crystal was thoughtful. For a moment or two Basil had sounded almost nervous. 'I don't think I would care for him at all. But he couldn't ruin you, Mr Corry, could he? You are too well established for that.'

Basil tried to speak lightly, but Crystal saw the fine line of perspiration along his forehead and her concern grew.

'No one is too well established to fall if Brummell so wills it.' Corry took out a spotless linen square, mopping his brow discreetly. 'No, no one's that secure. A single word from the Beau, my dear, and I'd be finished.'

Whilst Crystal worried about George Brummell and the possible harm he could inflict upon Basil Corry, Fanny Bethall was revelling in the joys and frustrations of her first love *affaire*.

She had taken to singing as she worked and spent more money on what Winnie Moloney called useless fal-de-rols. She wasn't reticent about her young man. Winnie and Crystal would exchange long-suffering glances as Fanny started another tale about Peter Heslop, who held her heart.

Heslop worked for a printer near Covent Garden. His wage was small and his work hard, but he didn't care. He was tall and well built, with dark curls and, as Fanny said many times, had the bluest eyes in the world.

As Fanny and Peter walked to the heights of Hampstead,

their favourite spot, both knew that marriage was an impossibility. Peter's father was dead, his mother an invalid, his eldest sister a dying woman. In addition, there were four other Heslops to support and it was often difficult for him to find enough money to buy bread and milk for the family. Taking a wife, and producing children of his own, was a venture as remote as flying to the moon. But neither he nor Fanny cared about their barren prospects.

In the few free hours they had together they held hands, looked into each other's eyes, and planned the home they knew they'd never have.

Lately, Peter had stolen the odd kiss or two, getting bolder when Fanny didn't resist. She loved the feel of his strong arms about her, but that was where it had to stop.

There was to be no funny business. The aristocracy might think nothing of sharing a bed with anyone who took their fancy, but that was not Fanny's way and she made it clear from the start. Peter accepted her decision, respecting her for it. He was rather proud of the stand she had taken, for he didn't want to walk out with a loose woman. Fanny was a virgin and he loved her the more because of it.

'I've got a bit o' money in me pocket,' said Fanny one dreamy spring evening as they watched the sun slip slowly down behind the gold-rimmed clouds. 'Ain't much, but mebbe it'll 'elp.'

Peter was uncomfortable, feeling his manhood threatened.

'I don't like takin' money from you, Fan; you knows that.'

Fanny understood him very well and had her answer ready.

'No one's offerin' *you* money, you great silly. It's for the young 'uns. They need plenty o' food inside 'em.'

'Well – ' Heslop hesitated and was lost. That morning

he hadn't a penny to buy a stale loaf for his hungry brood. It had eaten into his soul to see their eager faces crumple in disappointment when he had shewn them his empty pockets. 'Not much, mind.'

'Two and sixpence.'

'That's a fortune.'

'You'll soon find good use for it. Yer ma wants a comfort or two as well, don't she?'

Peter's head was bowed, the flush on his cheeks darkening.

'I could get a bit o' meat and make some broth for 'er and Beth,' he admitted slowly. 'But what about you? You need your wages for yourself.'

'All I'd do with 'em is buy another 'at at the market, I shouldn't wonder. And you never notice what I've got on me 'ead anyway.'

'Not with 'air like you've got, Fan. You ought never to cover that up.'

Fanny blushed with pleasure.

'Go on with you. You won't argue no more?'

'No, but it'll just be a loan.'

Both knew that Peter would never have enough to repay Fanny, but it helped to ease the awkwardness.

'O' course. Just a loan.'

They lay back on the grass, their bodies just touching, totally content to be in each other's company. They exchanged a few kisses, whispered of what colour their parlour carpet would be, then rose because their blissful interlude was over.

As they held each other for one last kiss, Fanny's normal gaiety and stout heart failed her.

'Oh, Peter, do you think there'll ever be a chance for us? I loves you so much.'

'And I you. As to our chances – ' Heslop shrugged.

'Mebbe things'll change one day. Ma says you ought never to forget that miracles sometimes 'appen.'

Fanny's smile was back and with it renewed courage.

'Yer ma's right and I'm a fool to doubt it.'

It was another piece of fiction, like the loan, but Fanny clung to it like a raft in a rough sea. If she let herself think of the future with clarity she would burst into tears and that wouldn't have been fair to Peter.

When she opened the kitchen door in Swan Street, Winnie was mending a stocking and Crystal painstakingly fashioning a tiny rose with a fine brush. They both looked up to greet Fanny. For a second she wanted to spill out her doubts and sadness to her two friends, but such weakness would bring the truth to the surface and she didn't want to face that.

'Well, luv? 'Ad a nice time, did you?'

Fanny got the cups from the dresser, starting to prepare the hot chocolate which they shared every night. She turned to Winnie, her eyes serene.

'That I did. My Peter gets more 'andsome each time we meet, I swears 'e does. Don't know what 'e sees in me, but I reckon I'm lucky to 'ave 'im, and that's a fact. Just let me 'eat the milk and I'll tell you all about what we did today.'

Mrs Moloney and Crystal shared a sigh as Fanny handed them their chocolate, bracing themselves to listen to Heslop's praises sung yet again.

'Well,' said Fanny as she sat herself down and took a sip of her drink. 'This is nice; I needed it after all that walking. Did I tell you what a good walker Peter is? Truth is, 'e's good at most things. Now, about this evenin' – '

Stuart Haversham stood by the window in the drawing-room of his parents' London house, his thoughts miles away.

Ten years had turned a good-looking boy into a strikingly handsome man with a flair for wearing clothes and an air of assurance every bit as marked as George Brummell's.

That morning he wore a perfectly tailored tail-coat of drab olive, tight-fitting pantaloons, and Hessian boots with a tassel to finish off their V-shaped dip in the front. His waistcoat was biscuit-coloured, his cravat a crisp work of art.

Despite his looks, his wealth, and all his privileges, Stuart was not a happy man. For some time he had been aware that he wasn't remotely in love with Charlotte Somerset. His mother had just spent the last half-hour pressing him to propose so that there could be a summer wedding, but the prospect of making Charlie his wife filled him with gloom.

The Marquis of Ravenmore watched his son in sardonic amusement. It was patently clear to him what was wrong with Stuart and he had noted the almost hunted look on Melfort's face as the latter had tried to stem his mother's urgings.

It was inevitable, of course. It was the marchioness and the Countess of Selkirk who had decided between them many years before that their offspring should marry. Whilst they were children, such plans made on their behalf hadn't mattered. Now they did.

'You're restless, Melfort,' said the marquis lightly. 'What's the matter with you?'

Stuart turned to look at his father who had grown more distinguished in middle age. A touch of grey at the temples enhanced his dignity; the light brown eyes were as keen and searching as they'd always been.

'I was thinking about love,' said Stuart, shaking off his depression as he moved into the room.

'Good God, boy,' returned the marquis in mock alarm.

'Whatever you do, don't do that. Being in love is worse than catching cholera.'

'I wonder if there is such a thing.'

Ravenmore gave a short laugh.

'You ought to know. You're almost engaged to Charlotte and you've scarcely led the life of a celibate for the past few years.'

'How do you know what sort of life I've led?' Stuart was faintly amused. 'You don't dog my footsteps after dark, do you?'

'Hardly. I've better things to do with my time. You don't flaunt your mistresses, I'll grant you that, but word reaches me nevertheless.'

'From that damned valet of yours, I suppose?'

'Herrick is useful, I admit, but even if he didn't exist, I doubt that I would remain in ignorance of what you do.'

'Damn it, my lord.' Suddenly Stuart was irritated. 'I feel like a child in a nursery with a nanny in attendance.'

Ravenmore gave a brief shrug of his shoulders.

'You're my heir and that's your bad fortune. I don't want you turning out like Rupert Somerset.'

'I hardly think that's likely,' retorted Stuart curtly. 'I neither cheat at cards, nor drink too much, nor – '

The marquis held up a protesting hand.

'Spare me a list of your virtues, I beg you. Why were you thinking about love? Have you met someone I don't know about?'

'Not yet.' Melfort's annoyance had evaporated. There wasn't a lot of point in being angry with his father. Ravenmore never took the slightest notice of such emotions. 'I don't suppose I ever will. Did you – No, I beg your pardon, my lord, I wasn't thinking.'

'Young bucks like you are seldom given to thinking, but the answer is yes. Once I was in love and, if your mother finds out, I'll know who let the cat out of the bag for no one apart from you and me is apprised of the fact.'

'You know I'd never repeat such a confidence,' said Stuart quickly, regarding his father in a somewhat different light. It was difficult to equate sexual desire with his austere parent. 'No, sir, the secret is safe with me.'

'I'm sure it is, otherwise I wouldn't have told you in the first place.'

'You said only you and I know of this matter, but there is the woman in question as well. Still, I suppose she would never speak of it.'

The marquis was silent for a while, Melfort trying to read what was behind the impassive mask.

'We only had a year together,' said Ravenmore finally, 'and then we parted. Our meetings were clandestine and not very frequent. But we didn't care. What we had was precious enough to transcend such disadvantages. Yes, Stuart, love does exist. However, take my word for it that you'll be happier without it. Marry Charlotte. You're fond of her and she won't put you on the rack.'

'But she won't arouse me to excitement.'

'Nor will she inflict pain, as I've just said.'

'It will be rather a pedestrian sort of life, won't it? I think I'd like to experience the real thing.'

'Doubtless you would, being a hot-head. I didn't really need to ask just now what was wrong with you. I already knew. You think of Charlotte just as a friend. Reconsider the matter; you could do a lot worse. Well, I can't stay here debating life and love with you. I've something far more important to do.'

'You're going to buy another horse.'

The marquis's lips twitched.

'I'm glad you're quick on the uptake, Melfort. I wouldn't have wanted a dullard for a son. Yes, I'm going to acquire a horse. They're so much more satisfactory than human beings, don't you think?'

And with that the marquis made a stately exit, leaving Stuart to return to the window and his growing doubts about a liaison with Charlotte Somerset.

Later that day, the earl's current mistress, Lady Laura de Vere, found him as absent-minded as his father had done.

'What on earth is the matter with you, Melfort?' she demanded when she had failed to move him with the sight of her flimsy wrap falling to the floor. 'I might just as well not be here for all the notice you're taking of me.'

'What?'

The earl came down to earth with a bump, seeing Laura properly for the first time that evening. She was a pretty widow of no more than twenty-three summers, with smooth, rounded limbs, large brown eyes, and a mouth which demanded kisses even when it pouted.

'I said – what is the matter with you? You appear to be sleep-walking and I don't think I shall find that very entertaining.'

Stuart pulled a face.

'I'm sorry. I shouldn't inflict my doubts on you.'

'What doubts?'

'Whether there is such a thing as real, enduring love to be found in this world.'

Laura gave an unladylike hoot of mirth.

'Melfort, you're out of your mind.'

'You don't think it exists?'

'Of course it doesn't. It's a fairy tale made up for mentally defective adults. There is sexual fulfilment and there is affection. You're chasing shadows, my lord. Stop being a fool and come to bed.'

'But if you're wrong – '

'Sir! If you have come here simply to talk to me as if I were your mother, then – oh!'

She gasped as Melfort picked her up and threw her across the bed.

'Be quiet, you witch. Whether you're right or wrong makes no odds at the moment. I know why I came here and so do you.'

Laura gave a lazy smile as Stuart pulled her into his arms, his lips a mere inch from hers.

'Well, you delicious strumpet,' he said very softly. 'What was that you said just now about sexual fulfilment?'

Three

Charlotte Somerset was finding Lady Cavendish's ball rather a bore.

Stuart was away for a day or two, but a suitable escort had been found for her in the shape of Lord Ellerdale. He was well mannered, well dressed, and as dull as ditchwater.

As she made polite conversation with a group of her contemporaries she had to admit that even if Stuart had been present her ennui would be just as strong. She had been certain for some time that she wasn't in love with Melfort. She was always glad to see him, and he was kindness itself, but he neither quickened her pulse nor made her yearn for the day when she would be his wife.

He hadn't actually proposed yet, but she knew he'd do so before long. She also knew she'd accept him, because she couldn't bear to hurt his feelings and, after all, there was no one else. Her friends were always telling her how fortunate she was to be the future Countess of Melfort.

'So handsome,' said one. 'So rich,' said another. 'And what style,' a third had said, adding a small dig about Lady Laura de Vere.

Charlotte knew all about Stuart's mistresses, for her acquaintances were prompt in letting her know when he moved from one spoilt darling's bed to another. It depressed Charlotte to find that she felt no jealousy or anger towards Stuart. If she had really loved him she would have been furious. As it was, she just hoped he would keep his *affaires* from the ears of her friends, once they were married.

Suddenly she was aware that her companions had dispersed and that she was alone. She was about to seek other company when Lady Cavendish bore down upon her accompanied by a tall man with dark hair and eyes.

'And you must meet Mr John Louis-Rey,' said Mary Cavendish in her high, trilling voice. 'I swear he hasn't danced once since he arrived. Charlotte, you must remedy that at once.'

She drifted away and Louis-Rey and Charlotte stared at each other for a very long time.

Louis-Rey took in the shining curls, cut à la Titus; the pale violet eyes under black lashes and the small, slightly tilted nose which gave the girl an oddly endearing look. Her mouth was generous and deep pink; her complexion as warm and perfect as a peach.

For her part, Charlotte was equally stunned. Louis-Rey wasn't really handsome. His face was too harsh, the nose too much of a beak, the cheekbones high, leaving deep hollows beneath them. His lips were well shaped but thin, his chin jutted just a bit too much.

Charlotte felt her heart sink. Louis-Rey might not have been an Adonis, but what he was doing to her was beyond question. Ludicrously, she wanted him to put his arms round her and bend to kiss her. She longed for every other person in the Cavendish drawing-room to vanish, so that she and this man who was gazing at her so unwaveringly could be alone. If Stuart couldn't make her pulse race, this man did it all too easily. He turned her knees to jelly and made her throat go dry with an emotion which she understood, although she had never experienced it before.

At last the silence had to be broken. They couldn't stand there, wrapped in naked desire. There were many sharp eyes about and with a calmness which did her credit Charlotte snapped the spell.

'Don't you like dancing, Mr Louis-Rey?'

'Not very much.'

His voice was low-pitched and it made shivers run up Charlotte's spine.

'We'd better try, I think. People may – '

'Yes, of course.'

John pulled himself together as they moved to the centre of the room. The feel of her hand against his made him light-headed and it took every ounce of his self-control to stop himself from pulling her closer and whispering of what she had done to him.

'I'm afraid Lady Cavendish's introduction was somewhat brief,' he said, his eyes still locked with hers. 'She said your name was Charlotte, but that's all I know about you.'

Charlotte swallowed hard. She didn't want to tell him about Stuart, but of course she would have to. The rules had to be obeyed, even though she had just fallen headlong in love.

'I'm Lady Charlotte Somerset. My father is the Earl of Selkirk, and before long I shall be betrothed to the Earl of Melfort.'

Louis-Rey saw the unhappiness in her even as the dull ache in his heart began. She was a million miles beyond his reach, yet he would love her until the day he died. He sensed her own reaction, too, and his manner grew cool for there was much danger for both of them.

'I see. My felicitations, Lady Charlotte.'

'Thank you.'

Her voice was small and she was near to tears. She had thought for one wonderful moment that he felt as she did, but she had been wrong. He was cold and remote as they finished the dance and made their bows.

When Rupert and his friends came up, Louis-Rey made his excuses, withdrawing as if he were glad to be rid of the duty thrust upon him by his hostess.

'Oh, Florrie,' said Charlotte as her maid prepared her for bed. 'I've met the man I would sell my soul to marry, but I don't think he even liked me. I was trembling like a leaf the whole time we were together, but he seemed relieved when he had the chance to leave me.'

'M'lady! What about the poor earl?'

Charlotte glanced in the mirror at Florrie's stricken expression and gave a wan smile. Florrie Bigland wasn't a lot older than the girl she served, and was very devoted. She was much more than a maid who brushed hair and made sure that gloves and slippers matched the gown of the moment. She was a close-mouthed confidante and one never had to pretend with her.

'I'll marry the poor earl, I expect, when he brings himself to ask me. I don't think he's any more in love with me than I am with him, but everyone expects us to wed. They'd tied the knot almost before we were out of our cradles. What a sad life we shall have. Stuart will seek solace in the beds of a dozen or more women, and I shall be dying inside because I can't be with John.

'You see, I already think about him by his Christian name, yet a few hours ago I didn't know he existed. I could have gone to the Marioness of Beresford's drum this evening. I was invited, but decided to go to the Cavendishs' instead. If only I'd made a different choice I'd never have seen John and I wouldn't be hurting so awfully now. Oh, Florrie! Why is everything so wretchedly unfair?'

If Charlotte had but known it, Louis-Rey was in equal torment.

'I shouldn't have gone to that blasted ball,' he said as he and his valet eased off the tightly fitting coat of dark blue superfine. 'I met a girl there I want more than life itself, but not only is she an earl's daughter, but she's betrothed to another of equal rank. She will have a title and wealth. I can't offer her either.'

'Beautiful was she, sir?' Angus Burns was mildly sympathetic. He wasn't much interested in women himself, believing them to be the root of all evil. But he was fond of his master, who was in a fair old state and quite unlike himself. 'Dark or fair?'

'Dark and exquisitely lovely.' The saturnine face was harsher than usual, tortured by the remembrance of the large violet eyes and a slender body which would have fitted against his own, as if God had fashioned them for each other, if the chance of such intimacy had arisen. 'I've never seen another like her and never will again.'

'Pity, sir; a great pity. Still, in my experience women do tend to have a disturbing effect.'

'Disturbing effect!' Louis-Rey was sour. 'Angus, you have a genius for understatement. I've just told you about a woman who has turned my world upside down, and made a weakling of me, and you say she is merely disturbing.

'Damn it! Why on earth didn't I go to Boodle's instead?'

On a bright morning in April, Crystal rose early. There was nothing about the day to suggest that it was to bring about the greatest of all changes in her life.

She took off her nightgown and folded it neatly. Then she washed from head to foot, refreshed by the coldness of the water. After that first bath in Swan Street she had been as fastidious as any fine lady in her toilet. The day's dirt cleansed away before retiring; night's ravages dealt with just as firmly.

There was a small pleasure to enjoy as she got dressed. A new muslin gown, with a high waist and graceful folds falling to her slippers. The gleaming red hair was pulled to the top of Crystal's head, secured by a narrow green ribbon and allowed to fall in soft ringlets.

The shop was busy that Wednesday. Basil was darting back and forth, trying to give each customer as much attention as possible. When he called to Crystal to bring in a tray of Benjamin's newly made silver boxes she took them to the nearest counter, still unaware of what was awaiting her.

She was vaguely conscious of a group of young fashionables, but it wasn't until she had set out Corry's treasures very carefully on a piece of velvet that she glanced up. Then she felt her heart miss a beat and her throat grow dry with something near to shock.

The man nearest to her was the most handsome creature she had ever seen, his splendid attire gilding the lily. She couldn't stop staring at him and eventually, as if her scrutiny had been like a touch on his arm, he turned his head to look at her.

Stuart had spent the previous evening with Charlotte. They had gone to Almack's, been favoured by a gracious nod from the gorgons who ruled that establishment with a rod of iron. They had danced, exchanged a few words with their friends, and partaken of the very inferior fare provided by the exclusive club. The whole thing had been flat and without satisfaction and, judging by the look on Charlotte's face, she hadn't been particularly happy either.

Now, looking at the girl with the green eyes, Stuart understood what had been lacking in his life. His father was right and Laura de Vere quite wrong. It was as if he had been struck hard in the solar plexus, and he knew without doubt in the first moment of their meeting that he was going to love the vision before him for the rest of his days.

It was the same for Crystal. He had had no knowledge of love, but she recognised it when it hit her like a thunderbolt. Her pulse was racing, her legs unsteady.

The look they shared seemed to go on forever. Then Crystal tried to bring back reality by re-arranging the boxes, only to drop one in her confusion.

It was Melfort who rescued it, his hand just touching hers. It brought renewed amazement to both of them and each had difficulty in preventing their fingers from linking with the other's.

'Thank you, sir.' Crystal was the first to force normality into the situation. 'I'm sorry I was so clumsy.'

Her heart was singing, her blood on fire, but at the back of her mind common sense was beginning to douse the magic.

The man whom she would never forget and never stop loving was clearly a rich aristocrat; she was a child from the slums of St Giles. This fleeting encounter would probably be the only one they would have and her initial joy was already turning to a deep sadness.

Stuart, reading her mind with ease, shared her depression. It wasn't simply that he was committed to Charlotte. Even if she hadn't existed, he couldn't have the woman who made him understand what passionate desire really meant. His father would never permit such a mésalliance.

'It's my pleasure.' He followed her lead, watching the lashes fall to cover the jewels which were her eyes. 'Perhaps you can help me.'

'I don't normally serve.' Crystal cast a quick look at Basil, still in debate with a particularly fussy customer. 'Mr Corry likes to do that himself.'

Stuart glanced over his shoulder and his smile made her weaker than ever.

'I think Mr Corry will be some time. Can we break the rules for once? I'd like to see some gold boxes, if I may.'

Crystal was in a trance as she led the way to a case where a few of Basil's French boxes lay in all their glory.

'These – these are very fine,' she said, finding it difficult to get her voice above a whisper. 'I'm afraid they're rather expensive, though.'

'I'm sure they are.' Stuart was regaining his own self-possession, although the way his goddess moved with such grace still bemused his senses. 'Old Corry's been raiding his godmother's collection again, I see. What is your name?'

The blush deepened on Crystal's cheeks.

'Crystal Yorke, sir.'

'And I'm Stuart Haversham. Tell me, have you – ?'

Whatever question the earl was about to put to Crystal was cut off abruptly as Basil bustled up, full of apologies.

'My lord, forgive me. Such a rush. I fear I've kept you waiting.'

'I have been well looked after. Miss Yorke has been most helpful.'

Basil smiled fondly at Crystal.

'Ah yes, of course. Now, something for your father, was it? I trust the marquis is well?'

'In rude health and yes, it's a gift for him which I'm seeking. His birthday is next week.'

Crystal's despondency increased. The fact that Haversham was the son of a marquis seemed to add to the width of the chasm between them.

'Of course, of course. Such a dedicated collector and quite as discerning as Mr Brummell.'

'A great deal more discerning,' returned the earl drily, 'and he's been at it longer. What about one of these? They're from reserve stock, aren't they?'

Corry's eyes twinkled.

'You're getting as astute as his lordship, but I think not these. I have something exceptionally rare put aside. I keep a note of some of my customers' birthdays and guessed you might be in before long. There – what do you think of that?'

Corry unwrapped the box which he had removed from a small drawer behind him, touching the delicate gold filigree and smoothing reverently the glowing ruby on the lid. There were tiny diamonds forming a bezel and more set into the sides. It was a work of art and Basil was justifiably proud of it.

'An exquisite piece.' Stuart's attention strayed back to Crystal for a second. The box was beautiful, but it couldn't hold a candle to the girl who had drawn back as if she didn't want to intrude upon the transaction. 'I'll take it.'

Melfort acknowledged Basil's bow and made his own to Crystal.

'My thanks, Miss Yorke. Corry, you ought to let her serve in the shop more often. She would pack it to the doors.'

When he had gone, Basil said reflectively:

'You have impressed the earl, my dear.'

'The earl?'

'The Earl of Melfort. I understand he will soon be betrothed to a woman of his own circle.'

There was only the slightest change in Corry's tone, but it was enough for Crystal to understand the warning.

'I see.'

'Yes, blue blood always marries blue blood. It's the way of the world, you know. Crystal, don't – '

Basil broke off, not sure how to go on, but Crystal straightened her shoulders, completely her own mistress again.

'I won't. As you say, blue blood marries blue blood and mine comes from tainted stock.'

'I didn't mean that. I wouldn't hurt you for the world, or see you hurt by another.'

Crystal managed a creditable laugh, light and uncaring.

'Dear Mr Corry, I'm not going to let myself be hurt, you may be sure of that. Don't you remember? I'm a survivor. Besides, he was just another customer, nothing more. Now, what about a glass of sherry before your luncheon?'

When Mrs Moloney heard that her friend, Mrs Green, was having one of her bad turns, there was nothing for it but the instant preparation of beef-tea.

'Nothin' puts Violet on her feet quicker than my special,' declared Winnie as she stirred the savoury brew with a vigorous hand. 'Now, Fanny, be a good girl and git down that jug. Then take this round to Mrs G. for me.'

It was dusk when Fanny left Swan Street, but she didn't mind that. She could pretend that Peter was walking by her side, just hidden from sight by shadows.

Mrs Green might have been having a turn, but it hadn't stopped her from gossiping. It was an hour or more before Fanny finally escaped, thanking her lucky stars that Winnie didn't prattle on like her friend.

Night had really descended by then, but there was a moon and Fanny hummed to herself as she cut through an alley-way towards Mr Corry's shop.

Rupert Somerset and his cronies, Sir Humphrey Possett and Lord Percy Sheffield, were far from sober. They had gambled heavily, lost, and drowned their chagrin in champagne, brandy and whatever else had come their way.

They were weaving their way unsteadily down the same alley as Fanny when they caught sight of her.

'Hey, Rupert.' Sheffield held on to the wall for support.

'There's a wench coming. Two thousand pounds says you couldn't mount her in your condition.'

Viscount Dunstone accepted the challenge without hesitation. He was still good looking, but even at twenty-four there were signs of dissipation in him. He had grown harder, more vicious and very devious with the passing of the years. He could still fool his mother and Charlotte, but the reputation he had earned for himself was known and frowned upon by many. Rupert always went just a bit beyond the pale and anxious mothers warned their susceptible daughters against having anything to do with him.

'Done, but make it three thousand.'

'Readily. A fool and his money are soon parted.'

'I'm not a fool.' There were ugly lines round Rupert's mouth. 'Watch your tongue, Sheffield, or I'll call you out.'

'Deal with the trollop first,' said Possett, belching loudly. 'One thing at a time, for Christ's sake.'

Fanny had no premonition of danger. She saw the men coming, prepared to stand aside for them, as they had grown near enough for the silver light to shew her their quality.

She was totally unprepared when Dunstone caught hold of her, screamed as he knocked her down and began to tear her clothing. She wrestled with him with all her strength until Rupert hit her in the stomach and then across the face. The force of the blows winded her and she sagged as he ripped her skirts up and sat astride her.

Fanny moaned, no longer able to defend herself. The pain being inflicted on her was excruciating, the shame even worse. She heard their voices loud in her ears, like devils taunting her.

'Come on, Rupert,' said Sheffield, lurching nearer to Dunstone's victim. 'Up and at her.'

'Yes, Somerset, she's only a common creature, anyone can see that. No need for finesse, m'boy. Give her something to remember you by.'

Fanny felt her molester thrust into her again, the agony sharper than ever. Then she fainted.

When she regained consciousness her mind was blank with terror and disgust. She seemed to be reliving the nightmare as somehow she crawled back to Swan Street and down the area steps.

Winnie took one look at her and turned the colour of whey, whilst Crystal rose from her chair just as pale.

'Fanny! Oh, my dear Fanny, what's happened? What is it?'

It took ten minutes to get the full facts from the now hysterical Fanny. Crystal, realizing the seriousness of the situation, had fetched Basil, who listened to his maid with growing anger and sorrow.

'Would you recognise any of them again?' he asked, when finally Fanny's sobs had subsided. 'Would you know them?'

Fanny's face was blotched and puffy, her eyes dead.

'No, sir, it were too dark, but I knows the name of the one what did this to me. One of 'is friends called 'im Rupert; the other called 'im Somerset.'

'Rupert Somerset.'

Crystal turned to look at Corry. She had never heard him speak in that voice before and it made her shiver.

'Do you know him, Mr Corry?'

Basil took a deep breath.

'I do; all of London knows him. He comes in here now and then, though I wish he wouldn't. He's a complete degenerate; not fit to live with decent people.'

'Then if you know him, we can – '

'He's Viscount Dunstone,' said Basil tightly, 'the Earl

of Selkirk's son. Who would believe Fanny's word against his?'

'But if he has a bad reputation as you say, surely – '

'There is still no proof. The other two men with him, whoever they were, would deny any charges we made on Fanny's behalf.'

'The way of the world?'

Crystal was bitter as she looked at Fanny's closed eyes.

'I'm afraid so.' Corry was containing his fury as best he could, not letting it inflame the anger of Mrs Moloney and Crystal. There was nothing he would have liked more than to make Rupert Somerset pay for what he had done, but he was too well versed in society's ways even to attempt such a venture. Fanny would merely be exposed to more contempt, and called a whore. Dunstone's innocence would be established by his companions. 'Get her to bed. If she needs a doctor, call one, but – '

Winnie Moloney hadn't been born yesterday either and she agreed with her master. There was nothing to be done, and bringing in a physician would rub salt into Fanny's wounds.

'That won't be necessary, sir,' she said briskly. 'Crystal and I can manage. 'Ere, Crystal, you take 'er that side and I'll go the other. When we've got 'er to bed, make 'er a nice strong cup o' tea with plenty o' sugar and I'll boil some water. There, there, Fan, it's goin' to be all right now, luv. We're 'ere to look after yer.'

Somehow they got the suffering girl to her bed, washed her, and made her drink the strong, sweet tea.

'I'd like to git me 'ands on the bastard what done this,' said Winnie softly as she saw fresh tears trickle down Fanny's face. 'I'd give 'im what for and 'e'd never want another woman as long as 'e lived. Wouldn't 'ave no use for 'er.'

After a while, Winnie went to her own room but Crystal sat by Fanny's side holding her hand. After about an hour, Fanny stirred as if she had come back from somewhere a long way away.

' 'Ow can I tell 'im?'

Crystal rose, brushing strands of hair from Fanny's hot brow.

'Tell whom, dear?'

'My Peter, 'oo else? What'll 'e say? 'E'll never believe me, will 'e? It's like Mr Corry says; my word against that brute's.'

'If Peter loves you he'll understand.'

'Don't think 'e will. I've allus refused 'im, you see. 'E didn't mind that, 'cos 'e knew why I wouldn't cheapen myself, but now – now I'm like any other street-walker.'

'Dearest, you're not. Of course you're not.'

'I won't tell 'im straight away.' Fanny's voice was slurred with exhaustion and a draught which Winnie had given her. 'Leave it for a bit, I think. Mebbe summat'll come to me so's I can – can explain – '

Crystal smoothed the covers over the sleeping girl and got into bed.

It was then she began to realise how Mr Corry, Mrs Moloney and Fanny had protected her for the past ten years. They had seen to it that no unpleasantness came near her. She had been sheltered and cared for, but the sight of Fanny's blood and her cries of torment brought the past back with a rush.

Fanny's ordeal was commonplace in Angel Court but she, Crystal, had forgotten that. She had let Basil and the others throw a blanket over the seamy, sordid, dangerous world of St Giles, but now that merciful blindness had gone.

The ugliness of life was still there, even in the select streets around Mr Corry's shop. A man didn't have to live in the stews to commit atrocities, nor be a low-born criminal to do foul deeds.

Crystal's cocoon had been ripped open and she knew that those who loved her could never repair the rent. She had to face things as they really were, not as Basil Corry would have them be for her.

'Fanny,' she said, knowing her friend didn't hear her. 'When you wake up I'll tell you about survivors. I'm going to be one whatever happens, and I'll make you one, too. Dear Fanny; we're both going to be survivors.'

The week following the attack on Fanny hadn't been an easy one for Crystal.

Fanny had needed much care and reassurance and Crystal had taken the opportunity of giving her a few lectures about rising above Fate's knocks.

She had managed to banish the memory of Angel Court from her mind. Dwelling on its miseries would do no good and in any event it was all in the past. She was now Basil Corry's assistant and she resolved to cling to the safety and respectability which that post brought her.

What was much harder to forget was the brief span of time in the shop when she had fallen in love with a man with hazel eyes whom she would probably never see again. His face was indelibly stamped on her mind and sometimes she thought she could still feel the touch of his hand against her own. At night, when Fanny was asleep, Crystal wept. As she worked, all her thoughts were of Stuart Haversham.

She was feeling very low on the morning when Basil asked her to deliver a special package to an old customer of his. She went upstairs, put on a leghorn bonnet trimmed with flowers, and then went out into the sunshine of Swan Street with her parcel.

The Earl of Melfort saw her leave the shop, torn between

relief and guilt. He had been waiting on the other side of the road from Corry's on and off for the past five days, hoping to catch a glimpse of Crystal. He had tried to make his head rule his heart. He had thought about Charlotte, who was to be his wife; of his father, who had strong views about the kind of mistress a man of rank should take. He also thought about the girl whom he loved and what harm he might cause her were he to walk back into her life.

He wasn't such a fool as to imagine that their relationship would be simply a matter of a kiss on the hand and a meeting of eyes which betrayed their love. He wanted to touch her, to feel her mouth against his, to hold her naked in bed, and possess her with all the lust she had aroused in him.

As she began to move out of sight, Stuart threw caution to the four winds. He soon caught her up with his long strides and was dazzled when the emerald eyes lit up to welcome him.

'Miss Yorke.' He raised his hat politely as if their meeting was the most casual of things. 'Would it be an intrusion if I were to walk with you?'

It was a crucial moment for Crystal, too, and she knew it. The sensible thing would have been to turn the earl away with a polite refusal. Then her life would continue safe and snug and without pain. It would also be empty, pointless and achingly lonely and the smile which Stuart was giving her was impossible to resist.

'Not at all, my lord, but I have quite a way to go. I hope that will not inconvenience you.'

'The longer the walk the better I shall be pleased.'

He fell into step beside her and then Crystal realised what a glorious morning it was. The sky was blue, ruffled here and there by a puff of white cloud; the sun shone on her curls until they burned like fire.

They didn't say a great deal. They were just content to be together, accepting the inevitable without using words.

'We could walk back through the Park,' said the earl tentatively when the delivery had been made.

'Yes, I suppose we could.'

'It's very pleasant there.'

'I know. I've been there often with Fanny.'

'Fanny?'

'Mr Corry's maid.'

For a second Crystal was tempted to tell the earl what had happened and to seek his help, but Fanny had pleaded with her and the others never to mention the attack. In a way Crystal was glad that she had made the promise. She knew she was being selfish, but she wanted nothing to spoil the wonder of the next thirty minutes or so.

When they were half-way through the Park they came upon a rustic bench under a clump of trees.

'Let's sit here for a while.' The earl took Crystal's hand and felt it tremble in his. 'There are things we have to talk about.'

'I mustn't be too long. Mr Corry will wonder what has become of me.'

'I won't make you late. Miss Yorke – Crystal – do you know what happened when we met the other day? And please don't make empty protests or avoid the truth.'

She turned her head, marvelling at his looks and what being close to him did to her.

'I wasn't going to. Yes, I know what happened. I'm not sure how I knew, because I've no experience of such things. I just knew that I'd fallen in love.'

Stuart gave a faint sigh.

'So did I, the very second I saw you.'

'It's rather awkward, isn't it?'

'I suppose it is, but I've never been happier in my life.'

'Neither have I, but what are we going to do about it?'
Stuart's smile faded.

'That's the problem. I cannot offer you marriage.'

'I wouldn't expect you to. Mr Corry says blue blood always marries blue blood. He said you were soon to be betrothed.'

'I am, and then whatever we share for the next few months will end for good.

'What will we share?'

'That's up to you. We could meet from time to time and walk in the Park. I could tell you that you're the most ravishing woman I have ever known and that I would give my life for you if needs be. I might even kiss the tips of your fingers and compliment you on your bonnet, but it isn't what I really want.'

Slowly Crystal stretched out one small hand to cover Stuart's.

'It's not what I want either.'

His sigh was much deeper that time.

'Do you understand the risks of becoming my mistress? Do you even know what it means? You are so young, so pure. If you become mine your innocence will be gone and you will suffer greatly when it all ends.'

Crystal laughed softly and Stuart closed his eyes. It was a sound which he knew he would remember always, even when he was old and no longer filled with the all-consuming heat of love.

'My lord, I spent the first eight years of my life in the stews of St Giles. I can recommend that as a quick way of losing one's illusions. Anyone who lives there is neither innocent nor ignorant. I know there will be danger and hurt, but it will be worth it.'

'Are you sure?'

'Yes I'm very sure.'

'I'll buy us a house, not too far away, but discreetly situated. I want you, my darling, I want you in my bed.'

'That sounds rather a comfortable place.'

'You won't get comfort.' Suddenly Melfort caught her by the shoulders, twisted her round, and kissed her with a violence which suprised even him. 'That is what you will get and more. You won't find me a tame lover. Possessing you will be no gentle act on my part.'

Crystal responded, swept away into a world which no one else could share, breathless when Stuart at last let her go.

'Well?' he demanded as she straightened her bonnet. 'Does that frighten you?'

'The only thing which frightens me is that I shan't be able to please you.'

'Oh, my darling! You needn't be afraid of that. When do you have some free time?'

'Tomorrow afternoon.'

'Then let's ride into the country. I don't think even I could purchase a house that quickly, but at least we'd be together. Can you be here by two o'clock?'

She nodded and then rose.

'I must run. Don't come with me, just in case we're seen. Tomorrow.'

Her smile was a benison, the kiss she blew him as she turned more valuable to him than all the gems on the marquis's snuff-boxes.

'Tomorrow, my lovely girl,' he replied, his heart full. 'Yes, tomorrow.'

Crystal seemed to float back to Swan Street as if reality was far away. When she reached the shop she forced the joy from her face, adopting a demure air as she went into the workroom to see what Benjamin Booker was doing.

'You've taken your time,' he said without looking up.

'What about them tools o' mine?'

'I'll do them at once; don't be cross with me. It was such a lovely morning I couldn't hurry. Oh, Benjamin, it really is a perfect day, isn't it?'

Four

It was a week before Charlotte saw Louis-Rey again. Reluctantly, she had agreed to attend a ball given by the Duchess of Amberly for her god-daughter's entry into society. Rupert escorted her, for their parents were in Ireland. Daphne was visiting a sick aunt who was rich enough for the Countess of Selkirk to bother about. Marcus was casting an appreciative eye over the bloodstock there. An ancient, but high-born, cousin had been installed in their London house for the sake of form, protecting Charlotte's reputation.

Also with Charlotte at the ball was Florrie. She was below stairs with the other maids and chaperones who had accompanied their young charges, having quite a good time themselves as the glittering assembly in the ball-room engaged in the Quadrille and Country Dance.

Charlotte wore a white evening gown, her dark hair carefully combed into artificial disarray, a jewelled bandeau sparkling under the lights.

It was when the Prince of Wales arrived that Charlotte noticed John. As the Prince joined the group he was in, Louis-Rey quietly and tactfully withdrew. He did not belong in the royal circle and had no wish to embarrass His Highness by forcing him to acknowledge a mere nobody.

Charlotte noted the humility and found it touching,

excusing herself from Lord and Lady Dessart and their
daughter. It was now or never and Charlotte was a girl of
spirit, used to making quick decisions.

'Good evening, Mr Louis-Rey. I had not thought to find
you here.'

John turned abruptly, caught off-guard for a second as
Charlotte's beauty cast a spell over him once more. The
desire was quickly hidden, but it was enough for Charlotte,
who felt peace and joy flood through her. He might look
forbidding now, but that brief moment was what mattered.

'Lady Charlotte.' He was very formal. 'I'm not quite sure
why I'm here. I don't really belong in such an exalted
sphere, but Viscount Corsham insisted that I should come
with him.'

'I'm glad he did.'

There seemed no answer to that and Louis-Rey tried to
fix his gaze on a silver urn, burdened with fresh flowers.
Charlotte gave a low laugh.

'We could go on meeting at such gatherings as this for
ever,' she said, half teasingly. 'We could talk of the weather,
or of the Prince's Pavilion at Brighton. Or we could be
truthful with each other.'

Louis-Rey was forced to meet her eyes again, his voice
chillier than ever.

'I'm afraid I have no idea what you mean..'

'Coward.'

'Madam?'

Charlotte gave a sigh, her amusement evaporating.

'Very well, I suppose I shall have to say it, for you seem
quite set on continuing the pretence. John, I knew I loved
you the first time I saw you. Are you going to put me down
and say it isn't the same for you?'

'I'm in no position to say anything.' He was fighting the
same battle as he had fought before. The desperate need to

take her in his arms and kiss her was growing harder and harder to resist. 'Your rank is already above mine. When you marry Melfort we shall be even further apart.'

'But I'm not going to marry Melfort.' Charlotte was wondering why the dark face above hers, with all its sharp bones and angular planes, seemed so wonderful to her. 'I'm very fond of Stuart, of course. We've known each other since infancy. It was then that our mothers decided that we should wed one day. It was nothing to do with what Stuart and I wanted. I was ready to accept him, when I was formally asked. Now that I know what real love is, I'm not going to throw away such heavenly bliss. Of course, we'll have to wait until mother and father get back from Ireland, and goodness knows how long that will be. But I can wait.'

'This is absurd,' said Louis-Rey shortly. 'I have absolutely nothing to offer you and I don't want Melfort calling me out. They tell me he's a first-rate shot."

'He is, but Stuart won't want to fight a duel with you. He's not in the least bit in love with me and I think he'll be only too thankful to be free of his obligation.'

'Your parents would never agree.'

John was trapped by the violet eyes, feeling himself being drawn into a situation over which he had no control. It wasn't only Charlotte's radiance which was weakening him. It was the love he saw in her which was so like his own.

'Mother may have hysterics but that can't be helped and I can handle father.'

'No! It's too ridiculous and you don't know how I feel about you. You haven't asked me.'

'I don't have to,' she replied softly. 'I already know.'

'Dear God! What a tangle.'

'Only if you make it so. I'll be riding in Hyde Park tomorrow afternoon about four. My maid is deaf, dumb and blind when she has to be. Be there, John, I want to see you.'

A refusal was on his lips when he felt her hand on his arm.

'I may be in the Park tomorrow. I'm not sure.'

Charlotte laughed, knowing she had won.

'You'll be there. Now ask me to dance.'

'You are a very forward young woman. I cannot think what kind of wife you will make.'

'Neither can I, but it will be fun finding out, won't it? John! You actually smiled at me then.'

'I've no idea why. It's not a smiling matter.'

'It's because you're happy, like me.'

'My only emotions at present are consternation and alarm.'

'Liar. Say what is in your heart.'

The music stopped and they made their bows.

'I must be mad,' said John helplessly. 'We've only met twice and all I know about you is that you are a bold hussy and talk too much.'

'And?' Her voice was tender. 'What else, my dear?'

'I love you.' He gave in, recognizing his defeat. 'God help me, Charlotte Somerset; I'm in love with you.'

It took the Earl of Melfort three weeks to find the house he wanted and to furnish it, but the lapse of time didn't bother him. He and Crystal were able to meet during her free hours and often when she was sent to deliver something he would appear miraculously at her elbow to escort her.

In many ways he was glad of the delay, for it gave Crystal time to get to know him better and to change her mind if she wanted to. But Crystal had no such intention. Every occasion they met she found she loved Stuart a little more, longing for the moment when she could be his.

She told him all about the snuff-boxes she was painting and it was hard for him to watch the almost childlike enthusiasm in her without reaching out to catch hold of her. She was like the breath of spring itself. Honest, open, eager and enchanting, she was a heady aphrodisiac to a man used to bored, world-weary females with no hearts.

Then one day Stuart gave Crystal a key, watching her eyes light up.

'Yes,' he said, the shadow of doubt still in his mind. 'It's ready, the house, I mean. The question is, my sweet, are you? Do you really know what I shall expect of you?'

Her hand closed over the small piece of metal which was to open the door to heaven for her.

'You asked me that once before. I told you I'd lived in the stews. I saw men and women copulate in the gutter in front of everyone. At least it won't be like that for us, will it?'

'Certainly not. I suppose it's because you look so untouched that I forget some of the experiences you've had. Still, you won't be an onlooker this time.'

The next afternoon Crystal explored the house as she waited for Stuart. It was a luxurious nest, filled with flowers, prepared with love.

When she reached the bedroom she paused. It wasn't fear of Melfort which sent a twinge of doubt through her as she stared at the silk-covered bed. It was the possibility that after the sophisticated women whom the earl had known, he might find her lacking in the qualities which would excite him.

'It isn't the same, is it?'

Crystal turned quickly.

'Stuart! I didn't hear you come in.'

'No, you were too deep in thought. Come and have some wine. One doesn't need to leap straight between the sheets, you know.'

'You're still afraid for me, aren't you?'

'A bit, but only because I love you so much and don't

want you to –'

'How kind you are. I hope you won't be so in bed.'

He looked up, frowning slightly.

'I don't understand.'

She smiled.

'You promised me you wouldn't be a tame lover and I'm holding you to your word.'

He took a deep breath.

'Very well; so be it. I just wish I could be absolutely sure that you're not doing this simply for my sake.'

'My lord, how can you be so blind? Are you going to undress me or do I have to do that myself?'

Slowly he walked towards her, looking deep into the green eyes. What he saw in them drove the last of his worries away and he laughed.

'Do you know, Crystal Yorke, I believe I've been quite mistaken about you. I think you may well prove to be the most delectable whore in London. And I am claiming the privilege of undressing you, so you'd better hurry up and finish your wine or go without.'

The excitement began for Crystal as he started to strip her. She was more aware of her body than she'd ever been before, glad that God had shaped it well for Stuart's pleasure.

When they lay naked on the bed, Crystal gave a small sigh.

'You were wrong about something else, too.'

He watched her stretch her arms above her head in hedonistic delight, feeling the first tingle in his loins.

'What?'

'The bed is very comfortable, whatever you may make of it later.'

After that the time for conversation was over. Slowly, Stuart began to stroke her satiny skin, his erotic touch quickening her breath and sending a shiver through her. Then she relaxed, eyes half closed, waiting expectantly for his next move. At first, their kisses were as light as butterfly wings, their arms and legs entwining as both savoured the feel of flesh against flesh.

When his hands grew rougher on her white breasts it sent a sharp thrill through her, nipples tightening in response, her back beginning to arch as the preliminaries came to an end.

As he whispered in her ear, his fingers moved downwards to where her virginity had lain unawakened until that moment. Quite unconsciously her hips took on a rhythm of their own, answering his increasing demands. With each second that passed the wild, carnal desire in her grew stronger as she surrendered to him without reservation. Her mind was blank, pure animal instinct swamping reason.

But it was when Crystal's hand found the organ of Stuart's manhood that the storm broke. Nothing was gentle then. Their hold on each other was fierce and greedy, their open mouths meeting in pure lust. They rolled across the bed and then to the floor in total abandonment, all restraints gone.

They were getting nearer to that perfect moment for which they were striving with every ounce of energy in them. The time when two human beings become one in the ecstatic wonder of perfect sexual satisfaction.

Although they were almost fighting now, each burning up as their rabid hunger all but consumed them, they knew that the goal they sought couldn't be rushed. That would only be reached when all things came together to make its arrival possible. They knew, too, that once the climax was upon them nothing could break it or turn it aside. The final moment of passion would become a torrent which neither would be able to control; an avalanche which would drown them in its sweeping current.

The raw craving in Crystal was an agony and she pulled Stuart closer, pleading silently for what she needed with every fibre in her. When she moaned in torment, the earl knew she was ready. A savage knee forced her legs apart. Then he thrust into her cruelly, as if to stamp his mastery upon her.

The miracle of her orgasm drew a cry of joy and disbelief from Crystal. She had not thought that such an exquisite sensation was possible for mere mortals and her senses reeled as she clung to Stuart, praying that the sorcery might go on forever.

Afterwards, they lay side by side, exhausted but triumphant. They had found, and made theirs, the ultimate peak of love, rejoicing in the brief glimpse of paradise which they had been granted.

It was some time before the silence was broken. They wanted to hold on to the mystical strands which still bound them, unwilling to return to a lesser plane of existence.

'Did I hurt you?' asked the earl at last. 'I expect I did, for you brought out a kind of madness in me.'

Crystal stirred lazily, propping herself up on one elbow, a wash of contentment and well-being flowing over her.

'Yes you did, but I wanted you to.'

Melfort smiled.

'I was right then. You are a wanton for all your innocent looks. And you, my very dearest dear. Was it all that you expected?'

'More – oh so much more. How could one imagine anything as marvellous as what we have shared? When can we meet again?'

He pulled her down against him, stroking the red curls damp with sweat which lay against her cheek.

'Thursday. When do you have to get back to the shop?'

'In half an hour or so.'

'Have you told Mrs Moloney and Fanny about us?'

'Not really and certainly not who you are. They've guessed I have a beau and they tease me about it, but very kindly. Winnie has warned me to be careful.'

'And you've ignored her.'

'And will again. How could she understand the gift you've given me?'

'What about Corry? Does he suspect anything?'

'I think so; he's very astute. I keep catching him looking at me in an odd fashion, but he's never said anything. I don't think he will. Basil isn't the sort of man to intrude on private things.'

'How will you explain things to them when it all has to end?'

'I'll find a way. Don't let's think about that now.'

'So little time.'

She was quick to comfort him.

'This is our life together. We are having to squeeze it into months instead of having the years most people enjoy. But it's so very right and beautiful.'

'And you are so brave. I shall want some of that courage when we have to say good-bye.'

'When you need it I'll have it ready for you. Meanwhile, my lord, do you realise that you haven't kissed me for nearly ten minutes?'

He let his sadness fade away. Crystal was right; this was a moment to treasure and the future seemed a long way off just then.

'Kisses are dangerous,' he said softly. 'Sometimes they lead to other things.'

'I'll risk it if you will,' she replied and put her arms round his neck. 'Dear Stuart, wouldn't it have been quite awful if your father had collected porcelain instead of snuff-boxes?'

*

It was two blissful months later that Viscount Dunstone, accompanied by Sir Humphrey Possett and Lord Percy Sheffield, paid a visit to Corry's shop.

They made polite bows to Brummell, who had arrived some ten minutes before, receiving a brief nod from the Beau whose mind was on the engraved box decorated with blue *basse-taille* enamel which he held in one hand.

As Dunstone and his friends reached the counter, Crystal came from the workshop with one of Benjamin's silver trinkets which Brummell had expressed a desire to see.

Rupert raised his quizzing glass and surveyed Crystal from head to foot. His stare was a near-insult and she felt her colour deepen. She would have gone on her way, but Dunstone stopped her.

'Here's a pretty thing, then,' he said. 'Never knew old Corry had it in him.'

Crystal kept her temper, but with difficulty.

'I am Mr Corry's assistant, sir. Now, if you will excuse me –'

'Ah, but we won't. Damn me, Possett, I swear if you dressed this wench up in the right finery she would fool anyone into thinking her a lady.'

'Sir! If you please.'

By then Corry, who had seen Rupert and his cronies, had hurried to Crystal's side.

'My lord, my assistant is busy. I will serve you.'

Dunstone leered.

'But not as well, I'm sure. I was just saying that one might almost think the girl well-born, for she has a haughty air about her.'

'Well, sir, that's as may be, but –'

Corry wasn't allowed to finish. Lord Percy Sheffield had lost heavily to Rupert at the tables a few nights before and was feeling vindictive.

'Since you're so sure, Dunstone, let's have a wager on it. Fifty thousand pounds say you couldn't introduce her into society without discovery of the deceit.'

'My lord!'

Crystal gave Corry a quick glance. Basil's face was very white and she could sense the fear in him although she didn't understand it. True, the three young beaux were being ill-mannered and tiresome, but had done nothing to cause the tremble in Corry's hands.

'Be quiet, Corry; hold your tongue.' Rupert had been caught napping by Sheffield. He hadn't got fifty pounds to his name, never mind fifty thousand. But he couldn't refuse the wager. Percy and Humphrey would make sure that everyone heard of his cowardice and he'd be a laughing-stock. He knew Sheffield was getting back at him for trouncing him at faro; Percy also knew that those winnings had gone in another reckless game the previous evening. Rupert was trapped but none would have guessed it. He eyed Crystal up and down again and nodded. 'Very well, Sheffield, you're on, only make it seventy-five thousand.'

'Done.'

At last Crystal began to see that the men were in earnest and told them roundly what she thought of their scheme. They took not the slightest notice of her as they went on discussing details as if she wasn't there.

But when Corry told them their breeding served them ill, Dunstone was stung to anger. He walked the length of the shop to where Brummell stood, the others watching as he spoke quietly to the Beau.

Rupert came back, an unpleasant smile on his face.

'I've put the wager to Mr Brummell,' he said coolly. 'He insists it be carried out. If you refuse, he will never enter this place again and neither will anyone else. You'll be ruined, or my name's not Rupert Somerset.'

Crystal's mouth dried, realizing at last the cause of Basil's fright. This was the man who had raped Fanny in such a brutal way. She had no doubts about the honour of Somerset. He was quite ruthless and unless she agreed to take part in his charade, all the long years of Corry's work would be finished. The Beau could end it; Basil had said as much. And now Brummell was supporting Somerset in his mischief.

She could hear Basil's tremulous protests, but she herself was steady again.

'For how long would this – this farce continue?'

'My dear, no!'

Basil was ignored again.

'Two weeks should suffice, eh, Percy?'

'I'll accept that.' Sheffield grinned, certain that the money was as good as in his pocket. 'Two weeks it shall be.'

'That's settled then; two weeks.' Dunstone was mildly surprised. The girl had bottom; there was no doubt about that. 'There'll be seven days to tutor you, of course. Three weeks in all.'

'Who's to teach her, Dunstone?' asked Possett idly. 'Goin' to do it yourself, are you?'

'Hardly. Charlotte will see to all that, of course. My sister's always game for a jape like this. Fortunately, our parents are away and Charlie's being guarded by the Duchess of Baverstock, a second cousin or some such thing. She's as old as Methuselah and deaf into the bargain. She'll be no problem.'

He looked back at Crystal, wondering what she was like in bed.

'Well, girl, what's it to be? Come, you'll enjoy it. Plenty of fine clothes and we'll lend you jewels the like of which you never dreamed of. You'll dance with the élite and dine like a queen. Or else you and Corry will starve in the gutter.'

'I won't allow it.' Basil was frantic. 'You can't do such a

thing.'

'But I can, m'dear fellow, and the girl knows it. What's your name, by the way?'

'Crystal Yorke, and I'll do it.' Her hand was squeezing Corry's arm to reassure him. 'After all, it won't be for long, will it?'

'No time at all and you won't get into any trouble because of it. We shall never explain who you really are. The mysterious noblewoman will appear and then disappear like a wraith. It'll be a talking point for weeks and we'll leave everyone guessing. Agreed Sheffield?'

'Absolutely, that is, if you succeed, which I doubt.'

'Crystal! You can't!'

'I'll have to.' Outwardly, Crystal was very calm. She was thanking God that Stuart had told her on the previous evening that he had to go to Scotland almost immediately. The Havershams had an estate near Loch Shinn in the Highlands and it was there that his mother had been taken ill. If he hadn't been leaving town she couldn't have agreed to Dunstone's plan, even if her refusal meant Basil's ruin. She and Stuart would have met at some ball or drum and she shuddered to think what might have been the result of that. But the earl wouldn't be in London and so at last she had a way of repaying Basil for all that he had done for her. 'Mr Corry, it is as his lordship says. It could mean the end of everything for you and I won't have that. And I'll be with the viscount's sister. You did say that, sir, didn't you?'

'I did. Don't worry, shopkeeper, I've no designs on your assistant this time. She'll have the strictest chaperone you could desire. That's it, except that before I go I'll have your oaths that not a word of this will pass your lips. Too much money rides on it. Swear to keep the secret, or I'll undo the pair of you.'

Sheffield and Possett had wandered towards the door,

but Rupert was making sure of his bet. His eyes glittered and there was an ugly line to his mouth as he struck the counter in front of him.

Basil was numb as he made his promise and Crystal's mind chaotic as she followed suit. It had all happened so suddenly. One minute the morning had been as normal as any other; the next she had found herself face to face with Rupert Somerset, forced to accede to his outrageous demands.

'You'll be sent a message in a day or two as to where and when you are to join my sister. And remember; keep still tongues in your heads.'

Corry and Crystal watched Rupert join his friends on the pavement, Basil near to breaking point.

'My dear, my dear, you can't do this. You know what sort of creature Somerset is. Fanny should be warning enough for you.'

'He doesn't want me.' Crystal was still composed, still comforting her distraught employer. 'It's the money he's interested in. I shall be safe with his sister. She isn't like him, is she?'

'Lady Charlotte? No, no, not a bit. She's a spirited girl and likes practical jokes, so I'm told, but people speak well of her.'

'Then you need have no fear for me.' Crystal made an effort to lift Corry's dread. 'Maybe I'll enjoy dining like a queen, who knows? As for Mr Brummell –' She turned to look at the man who had made the viscount's threat possible. 'Beau by name but not by nature. How I hate him! Mr Corry, how could he do such a terrible thing to you?'

Five

'Really, Rupert, why do you remain friends with Percy Sheffield? He leads you into such bizarre situations.' Charlotte had just finished dressing for dinner when her brother appeared to tell his tale. 'As for this latest idea, I'm not sure that I want to be bothered.'

'Charlie, you'll have to.'

Charlotte heard an unexpected note in Rupert's voice and turned from the mirror.

'Why?'

'Because I've made a bet on our success.'

'A bet? How much?'

'Seventy-five thousand pounds.'

Charlotte gasped.

'But you haven't got seventy-five thousand pounds.'

'Don't I know it. That's why I've got to win.'

'You are too reckless by half.'

'Don't lecture me, for Christ's sake.'

'Someone ought to. What would father say?'

'He won't find out. You'll help me and you'll give me your word that you won't tell anyone about this. A careless moment and the whole world would know the girl's a fraud before we start.'

'What does she say?'

'She's agreeable.'

Rupert kept a steady gaze on his sister. He hadn't mentioned the existence of Basil Corry, or the ruse he'd used, making Brummell his unwitting tool. Charlie would never have stood for that, nor would she agree unless she were certain the Yorke woman was really willing.

Charlotte still hesitated. She wasn't enthusiastic about her brother's ridiculous escapade. She wanted all her time to think about John. Still, Dunstone was in a tight corner, for her father had very emphatic things to say about men who failed to pay their gambling debts. In the end she shrugged her acquiescence.

'All right, but you're a nuisance, Rupert.'

'You'll do it, though?'

'I've just said so. Now go away; Florrie will be back in a minute. Florrie! Oh botheration! We'll have to let her in on it. How can I transform your guttersnipe into a lady without Florrie's help?'

'Can you trust her?'

'Implicitly.'

'Very well, but not another soul. And you promise your silence?'

'For heavens sake! Of course I do.'

The viscount relaxed and grinned.

'I knew you'd do it. You're a good sport.'

'And you're an idiot, but I still love you. Oh, Rupert, Rupert, when are you going to grow up?'

On the following day Crystal and Stuart met to say good-bye.

'I had another note from my father today,' said the earl, winding one of Crystal's curls round his finger. 'Mother seems to be worse. It may mean I'll be gone longer than I expected.'

Crystal held her breath.

'How long do you think?'

Father advises me not to make any arrangements for the next month. I'm sorry, darling.'

'It doesn't matter; it doesn't matter in the least.'

The vehemence of her reassurance startled him.

'You sound as if you're glad to be rid of me.'

Crystal turned to him in dismay.

'You know I'm not. It's just that I'm sorry to hear about your mother and I don't want you to worry about me.'

'I see.'

The earl searched the wide green eyes and found no satisfaction in them. Crystal was different that evening. Some of the heart-stopping joy had gone out of her and she seemed preoccupied. Twice he had had to repeat a question and it bothered him.

'If something were wrong you'd tell me, wouldn't you?'

Crystal realized her carelessness too late, seeking feverishly to mend fences.

'Of course I would, but nothing is wrong. I swear it. Tell me what you've been doing today.'

'Not much.' Melfort was still unconvinced by Crystal's protestations, but he was prepared to wait to discover the cause of the change in her. 'I rose late, breakfasted with Brummell, and then – Crystal!'

He could feel her trembling as he caught her by the shoulders. The quiver of her lips had soon been brought under control, but he hadn't missed it.

'Yes?'

'There is something. What is it? Good God, I'm not a stranger to me kept in the dark.'

'I know, I know, but I'm perfectly all right.'

'Yet you shake when I tell you I was late rising, or was it George's name which disturbed you?'

'George?'

'Brummell.'

'Of course not, how could that be? I don't know him, that is, he's been to Mr Corry's shop, but I've never spoken to him.'

'Then I don't understand.'

'There is nothing to understand. Stuart, don't let's waste this evening. You're imagining things.'

But the earl knew he wasn't. Even when finally they made love it wasn't the same as usual. He made no comment on the fact, troubled by Crystal's pallor.

'If you're ill –'

'But I'm not – at least –' Eagerly she seized on a way out. 'Well, to tell the truth I think I've taken a slight chill. I didn't want to say anything and weary you with my petty ailments, especially on our last night. I shall have some of Winnie's special beef-tea and then I'll be fine again.'

He believed her because he wanted to, thrusting aside a tiny lingering doubt as he took her face between his hands.

'Never stop loving me, Crystal.'

'I won't.' She let the viscount's devilment fade from her mind. 'For as long as I live I will love you. You are all that matters to me; all that will ever matter however long the years may be.'

That time her kiss felt right to him. She was wholly his, nothing dividing them. He chided himself for doubting her. With her body close to his, her lips against his own, he was utterly and completely content.

'Chill or no chill, my beloved, we shan't see each other for a while. Shall we now make our farewells properly? Oh, my dear, dear girl. I do need you so very much.'

'Heavens! Rupert didn't tell me you were a beauty.'

Charlotte's initial reluctance to help her brother had quite faded. Louis-Rey had had to go to Cornwall for a while to deal with problems connected with a small estate he had there. Charlotte missed their secret meetings intolerably and was rather glad to have some diversion to fill what would otherwise have been long, empty days.

In addition, her penchant for practical jokes had reasserted itself. She was looking forward to fooling some of her more pompous acquaintances, not least the cabal which ruled Almack's. The delicious mystery which would linger on after the mysterious stranger had vanished would be almost as much fun as presenting her to the nobility.

'Thank you, Lady Charlotte.'

Charlotte gave Crystal a longer and more searching look. The girl's face was expressionless, the voice chilly. Yet Rupert had sworn Miss Yorke had been willing to take part in the deception and Rupert had never lied to her before. Charlotte put it down to nerves on Crystal's part, dismissing her doubts. It was rather a daunting prospect for a girl from humble surroundings to be faced with the full panoply of the *beau monde* and Charlotte set about putting her pupil at ease.

'I didn't want to do this at first,' Charlotte confided to Crystal as she indicated a seat by the window. 'I thought it would be rather a bore, but I've quite reversed my opinion. I've always been a monster where practical jokes are concerned. My brother and I used to do the most dreadful things when we were children.'

Crystal stole a look at Lady Charlotte. She wasn't in the least like her brother in appearance and her manner was warm and friendly. Oddly, Crystal sensed at once the decency in her mentor-to-be, not understanding how she could lend herself to blackmail with such a light heart.

'Don't look so serious.' Charlotte was still trying to break through the almost tangible barrier between herself and her guest. 'You've no need to be afraid. I'll teach you everything you need to do and you'll play your part splendidly, I'm sure.'

The niggle of doubt increased when Florrie came in and was duly introduced. The maid had the same openness of countenance and kindliness as her mistress, but it was too early for Crystal to make judgments.

It was after three days of intensive instruction, leavened with laughter, during which Crystal was treated with utmost courtesy and care, that she finally realised what had happened. Lady Charlotte was clearly unaware of the viscount's threats and equally ignorant of the fact that his pawn was an unwilling party to his scheme. Somehow, Dunstone had fooled his sister into believing it was just one of those practical jokes of which she was so fond.

Crystal couldn't tell Charlotte the truth; she had given her oath to Dunstone to keep silent. If she were to breathe one word the viscount would be sure to learn of the broken promise and then Basil Corry and his business would be finished.

It was unfair to keep Lady Charlotte at arm's length and treat her with such hostility when she was totally innocent of any misdoing and Crystal's anger melted as the lessons went on apace. Dressmakers came and went; shoes, fans, reticules and other frivolous pieces of nonsense were delivered in shoals.

Once, she ventured a comment as to the cost of it all, but Charlotte, relieved that Crystal was at last over her nerves, waved a dismissive hand.

'There'll be plenty of money to pay for them after you've made your debut. Don't worry about it. You're doing so well I hardly need to tell you much else. Frankly —'

The two girls were alone, Florrie busying herself in the next room laying out more clothes. They were drinking hot chocolate and the moment was ripe for confidences.

'Yes?'

'You'll think me very rude, but I hadn't expected anyone like you. You've had a good education, that is clear, and your diction is faultless. From the way Rupert spoke, I thought you would be – well – rather common. How awful that sounds; forgive me.'

Crystal's mind winged back to Angel Court, wondering what Charlotte would say if she knew the whole story, including the part the Earl of Melfort played in it. But if Charlotte could afford to be expansive, Crystal could not. She merely murmured something about no apology being necessary, vaguely referring to a Dame School which was rather out of the ordinary.

'Well, in two days the sport will begin.' Charlotte put her cup down with a smile. 'Rupert says you are to be introduced as Lady Jane Markham, sister of a friend of his who is abroad. Upon arriving in England your chaperone was taken ill and I agreed to take you under my wing, with the approval of the Duchess of Baverstock, although that old dear knows nothing of our plans. No one will question you; you'll see.'

And no one did. Crystal's first appearance at a ball, escorted by Rupert and Charlotte, caused a minor sensation. Diamonds nestled in the carefully dressed hair; the lute-string gown revealed enough of Crystal's shapely body to make the most hardened roué sweat a little.

People commented on her charming manners and the poise with which she accepted adulation. She was an instant success and whilst Charlotte crowed with delight, Dunstone's fear of losing the bet lessened with each hour that passed.

Much as she hated the role into which she had been forced, Crystal was human enough to enjoy wearing fashionable gowns and jewels borrowed from Charlotte.

She attended routs, balls and banquets; rode in Hyde Park in Charlotte's magnificent equipage, and each evening joined the throng of the élite as it moved from one house to another in a string of carriages drawn by the finest horses and attended by liveried footmen.

When the last evening came, Crystal sighed with relief. It hadn't been quite as bad as she had expected. She and Charlotte had grown fond of each other in the past three weeks; Dunstone had almost won his bet, and the danger to Corry was drawing to its close.

On the final evening Charlotte introduced Crystal to Brummell. It was the Beau who had turned men away from the highly coloured silks and brocades of the Macaronis and decreed that clothes must be simple, unobtrusive, of best material and impeccable cut.

That evening he wore a dark blue tail-coat, fitting like a second skin, white waistcoat, with black pantaloons buttoned tightly to his ankles over stockings of striped silk.

The Beau was disposed to be gracious, complimenting Crystal on her appearance. He, and those gathered round him, expected a quick blush of pleasure or a shy stammer of thanks for such a favour. Instead, Crystal just stared Brummell out, a sudden silence falling over the group.

Brummell was perplexed. It wasn't simply that he was used to a different reaction to his hard-won praise. There was a positive dislike in the green eyes and something else which he couldn't read.

He gave the girl a further moment to respond, but she did not take advantage of her second chance.

Then he raised his eyebrows in a way well known to everyone present, his drawl more pronounced than usual.

'At first I thought it was a trifle warm in here,' he said, taking a pinch of snuff with a graceful twist of one wrist. 'Now that we have an Ice Maiden in our midst no doubt we shall all be shivering before long.'

As he walked away, Charlotte said in a horrified whisper:

'What can you be thinking of? Did I not warn you to be careful how you spoke to the Beau?'

'Perhaps. I must have forgotten.'

'It was more than that, wasn't it? You looked as if you loathed him, but you've never met him before, have you?'

'No, nor do I wish to do so again.'

'Well.' Charlotte raised her hands helplessly. 'I confess myself at a loss and it's as well your task if all but over. You've made a bad enemy there.'

Crystal's smile was without humour.

'I don't doubt it, but this is my last night as Jane Markham so what does it signify?'

'Nothing, I suppose, but I'd still like to know – oh, never mind. It doesn't matter. I must go and speak to Lord Welton. Don't stray far, for we're all going on later to play cards at Lady Mercier's.'

George Brummell watched Crystal from across the crowded ballroom. Something had been bothering him since she had tried to freeze him with her stare. At first, he had been extremely annoyed, but somehow the pique had now quite gone. He wasn't sure what had caused the incident, but it chafed on his mind for a full hour before the answer came to him. The Ice Maiden had exhibited contempt, but behind that there was great pain in her as well. Yet surely he couldn't have been the cause of either the anguish or the rage. He'd never set eyes on the wench before.

'A penny for 'em, George.'

Brummell turned and raised his quizzing glass, letting it wander idly over Lord Beaumont's portly figure.

'If you are offering me a penny for my thoughts, Charles, you're a bigger fool than I took you for. My thoughts, like everything about me, are exclusive and not for sale. And talking of folly, m'dear fellow, where in the name of God did you get that extraordinary coat?'

No sooner had Charlotte disappeared into the throng than their hostess, Lady Brockenhurst, descended on Crystal in a flutter of white muslin.

'My dear, you must meet the Earl of Melfort, just back from Scotland. My lord; Lady Jane Markham. She has been with us for such a short time, yet she has every man in the room sighing for her. Tell her about Fort Ullen, Stuart. Such a lovely place set in those heavenly Highlands. I must go and rescue my poor husband from that tiresome Venables woman.'

Crystal felt as if she turned to stone. She hadn't noticed the earl approaching and had had no time to prepare herself for what was to come. Stuart's face was like a mask, his eyes as inimical as the line of his mouth.

'Lady Jane Markham?' His voice was clipped. 'How strange. I could have sworn I knew you by another name but, of course, I must be mistaken.'

'My lord, I –'

Crystal couldn't get any more words out but it made no odds. The earl had taken her arm in a grip of iron and was steering her towards one of the ante-rooms. When the sound of voices, laughter and music was cut off he said curtly:

'Can you explain any of this in a way which I would find even remotely believable?'

Crystal's dry lips parted, but she could feel the cords of her vow strangling her into a dreadful silence. Melfort was caustic.

'No, of course you can't, but perhaps I can. You are a cheat and a fraud and always have been. What did you hope to get out of this? A rich and titled husband?'

'No!'

'There can be no other reason. You have fooled people into accepting you as a lady, when you are no more than a girl from the slums with a burning ambition.'

'That isn't true.'

'I think it is. I gave you a taste for my kind of life. You knew I couldn't marry you and so you decided to amuse yourself with me and then seek more fertile ground. I should have realised that your agreement to become my mistress was too quickly given. How you must have been laughing at me when I professed my love for you. And now I see why you were so relieved to learn that I was going away.

'You were unfortunate; my mother is temporarily better so I was able to return to London. I imagine you'd given yourself the month you thought I'd be at Fort Ullen to pick yourself a wealthy and gullible fool. Perhaps you've already succeeded and received an offer.'

'No! I –'

'No? Ah, you needed the extra week, eh? What an unpleasant shock it must have been to you to find me here tonight. You are unlucky, but life is like that. Those who gamble for high stakes are always at risk. Damn you! How could you have done this to me?'

Crystal could see the fury in Melfort mounting, trying to stem its flood before it overwhelmed her.

'It isn't what you think, truly it isn't. I don't want a husband, rich or otherwise. I only want you.'

'Don't add another lie to all the rest. If you really wanted me you wouldn't be here now, wearing your fine feathers.'

Crystal could feel the tears beginning to well up behind her eyes, but she wasn't going to break down in front of Stuart, nor let him see what his scathing accusations were doing to her.

'I can't tell you how this came about. I wish I could, but

is it not in my power to do so. If you love me, you'll trust me.'

'Love! You don't even know what the word means. To you, what we shared was the satisfying of an appetite, nothing more. I thought you were a virgin but, of course, there are ways of faking that condition as both of us know. As for trusting you –'

'Don't! Oh please don't.'

'Why not? Are you the only one entitled to inflict hurt?'

'No, but I didn't mean to –'

'I believe you did.'

'I swear –'

'Good-bye, madam.' Melfort was frigid. 'We shall not be meeting again and if you shew yourself in town after tonight I shall expose you. You've lost the game and no friend or acquaintance of mine shall suffer as I have done.'

Helplessly, Crystal watched the door close. Fate had been so cruel. If Stuart had remained in the North for one more day all would have been well. He would never have known what happened for, even if people talked of the strange appearance and disappearance of Lady Jane Markham, he wouldn't have connected her with the name. Even the unspeakable Dunstone had said no one would ever be told the true story.

As it was, the earl's scalding wrath had poured over her like boiling oil, searing her very soul. For one moment she considered rushing after him and telling him the whole truth. Then she knew it would be useless. He wouldn't believe her now and, in any event, there was still Basil to think about.

She walked to the door, drained and empty. She would never see Stuart again; never feel his touch, or exchange a kiss with him. They wouldn't lie together in passion any more, or talk of sweet intimate things when their love-making was over. He had gone out of her life for good, convinced that she was a cheap strumpet who had simply wanted a rich lover whilst she set about finding a spouse.

And there was something else, equally devastating, which she had to think about.

'Crystal, where have you been?' Charlotte was at her side, shaking her out of her nightmare. 'I thought you'd been spirited away. Rupert and I and the others are ready to leave for Lady Mercier's. Are you all right? You look as if you'd seen a ghost. There's nothing to worry about now. By two a.m. Rupert will have won. You've been quite marvellous. I don't know what we'd have done, if you hadn't played your role so well.'

'My deceitful role.'

Charlotte heard the flat note in Crystal's voice.

'Well, yes, perhaps, but it was only a bit of fun and tomorrow you can be yourself again. Lady Jane is almost dead.'

Crystal wanted to scream that the part she had been forced to play had cost her Stuart's love, but there was no point. She could still feel the earl's hatred shrivelling her skin and making her heart pound.

'Yes,' she said dully, seeing her companion's head tilt in enquiry. 'Lady Jane will be dead, but she may not be the only one to go.'

Charlotte frowned, not liking the look on Crystal's face.

'What can you mean?'

Crystal was thinking of the disaster that had befallen her, which she now had to overcome without Stuart's help.

'Crystal Yorke may not die, Lady Charlotte,' she said finally, 'but one thing is certain. After this, she will never be quite the same again.'

Six

Lady Mercier's establishment was a revelation to Crystal. Just before the dawn of the new century, a number of titled women had created a scandal by keeping a faro bank at their houses. A few had now given up in the face of public disapproval. Lady Mercier didn't give a fig for anyone's opinion and gambling for very high stakes continued to take place in her house every night.

Charlotte had given Crystal some money, sitting by her side and instructing her how to play. By midnight, Crystal had accumulated a very handsome sum, staring at her winnings in bewilderment.

'Beginner's luck,' said Charlotte with a laugh. 'Come along; it's time we went before Dame Fortune begins to frown on you. Here, put the money in your reticule and don't leave a sou for old Virginia Mercier. She makes a small fortune running this place as it is.'

Rupert's party moved on to another house. No gambling that time. Merely an exchange of gracious nods or a word or two. It was just a question of seeing and being seen.

As they descended the stairs, Crystal found herself next to Dunstone, Charlotte ahead of them and out of earshot.

'I've kept my part of the bargain,' she said, Stuart's angry face still in her mind's eye. 'Now are you going to keep yours and let me go? And leave Mr Corry alone, too, of course.'

Dunstone was feeling remarkably cheerful. He had won at Lady Mercier's and very shortly he could claim seventy-five thousand pounds from Percy Sheffield.

'Of course. In two hours you can go on your way, shop-girl. Corry's safe for the moment. Meanwhile, stay close to me.'

At yet another house, some half-hour later, Charlotte encountered Stuart. She saw the whiteness of his face and the fury in him and was filled with concern. She had never seen him in such a state before and she could not leave him like that.

He protested as she drew him downstairs and into the garden, where coloured lights strung between trees lit up the sleeping flowers.

'Stuart, what is it? Is it your mother?'

'No and I don't want to talk about it.'

'But you must. Something terrible has happened to you; I can tell. My dear, you can trust me.'

By then they had found a rustic bench, the earl reluctantly taking a seat beside Charlotte.

'It's not a matter of trust and you're the last one with whom I wish to discuss the affair.'

'Then it concerns me?'

'In a way.'

'Then I have a right to know. Come, Melfort, do we have to sit here all night while I try to persuade you as if you were a fractious child?'

The earl took a deep breath.

'Very well, but don't blame me if it hurts. Do you know the woman who calls herself Jane Markham?'

Charlotte felt the first premonitions of danger creeping along her nerve-ends.

'Markham? Why yes, everyone knows her. She hasn't been in London for long, but –'

'She's a trickster. Her name is Crystal Yorke and, until she forced herself into places she had no right to be, she worked in a shop.'

Charlotte maintained her sang-froid, even managing to sound surprised.

'How do you know this? You'd gone to Scotland before she arrived.'

'I didn't want to distress you, but you've persisted so it's on your own head. She was my mistress.'

Charlotte was aghast, her hands tight about her fan so that they shouldn't betray her shock by trembling.

'Your – your mistress?'

'Just so. I'm sorry, but you did ask. If I'd thought you were in love with me I wouldn't have admitted my relationship with this trollop, but I'm sure you're not.'

'How long –?'

'About two months or so and then, as soon as my back was turned, she set about trying to entrap some wretched man to make him her husband. Well, she won't do that now. I've warned her that if I see her in town after tonight, I'll tell the whole world who she is and what she's done.'

Charlotte didn't know how she managed to sit by Stuart's side with such apparant poise. If she had known Crystal was Stuart's mistress, nothing Rupert said would have made her party to the wager. She wanted to tell the earl everything, but she wasn't sure that the hour had come when she could speak so freely.

'What time is it?'

Melfort consulted the jewelled watch in his pocket.

'One o'clock. Why?'

'Oh nothing, nothing. I just wondered.'

Charlotte's mind was racing with new fears. She couldn't breathe a word, even to Stuart, until the hour of two had come and gone. He would have exposed the whole thing

immediately and then Rupert would owe Sheffield a large
sum of money which he couldn't pay. She had promised her
brother her silence and she had to keep her vow. But for the
first time doubts were assailing her as to Crystal's part in
Rupert's plan.

If Crystal was in love with Stuart, was it likely that she
would willingly lend herself to such a deception, knowing
the earl might return to London at any time? That first day
when they had met, Crystal had been so cold. Had it been
mere nerves or something else? Although Charlotte was
devoted to Dunstone, she wasn't entirely deaf to what was
said about him. Crystal might have thought that she,
Charlotte, was made in the same mould as Rupert.

She wished with all her heart that John was there, so that
she could pour out her fears to him and seek his guidance.
But Louis-Rey was still away and she had to deal with the
problem alone, at least for the time being.

'Are you going to say anything, Stuart?'

'Of course not.' He was short. 'I've been made to look
foolish enough. If she were to continue with the
masquerade I would, but somehow I don't think she will.'

'Neither do I.'

Charlotte's rejoinder was soft, but it made Stuart look at
her properly for the first time.

'Do you know anything about this?'

The lie was bitter on Charlotte's tongue.

'No, of course not. I just meant that in her place I
wouldn't stay. Stuart.'

'Yes?'

'You said you didn't think I was in love with you.'

Suddenly the earl's rage subsided.

'Charlie, I'm sorry. I ought not to have said that, nor told
you the Yorke woman was my paramour. It must have been

like a slap across the face for you. Forgive me.'

'Willingly and you don't know how relieved I was when you made your confession.'

'Oh?'

'Yes, you see I'd been thinking of ways of telling you something without hurting you, but I simply couldn't find the words. Now you've found them for me.'

'I'm not sure I know what you're talking about.'

For the first time Charlotte managed a smile.

'You were in love with Crystal, weren't you?'

'I thought so.'

'No, Stuart, you were, or you wouldn't be aching as you are now.'

'All right. I was a buffoon in love, what of it?'

'Well, it's the same for me, my dear. I've fallen in love, too. I didn't mean to, but it just happened. May I tell you about my dearest John?'

The earl studied Charlotte's happiness for a moment or two.

'I think perhaps you'd better, don't you?'

He listened to Charlotte's breathless account of her meeting with Louis-Rey and her undoubted devotion to him. He found himself envying her. The one she adored had not betrayed her as Crystal had betrayed him.

'Do you mind very much?' asked Charlotte finally. 'I'm not doing you a great wrong, am I?'

'Of course not, Charlie. The wrong would have been if you'd married me whilst in love with another man. You're free as far as I'm concerned. What about your parents?'

'They're still in Ireland, but as soon as they're home I shall tell them about John. And now I must go. Rupert and the others will wonder where I am. What is the time now?'

Melfort frowned.

'You seem unduly interested in the hour. Why is that?'

He saw her flush, but she gave him no more time for questions.

'I'm truly sorry about what has happened,' she said as she blew Stuart a kiss. 'I'm sure you'll get over it soon.'

The earl watched Charlotte flying over the grass, his lips thinning.

'No, I won't, my dear, no I won't. I'm going to love that treacherous little bitch until I go to my grave. Oh damn you, Crystal Yorke, damn you to hell!'

'Well, it's over.'

Basil Corry looked at Crystal's strained face doubtfully.

'Is it?'

'Yes, the viscount's won his bet and I'm free.'

'I wonder.'

Crystal didn't look at Corry.

'I've something to give you,' she said and began to empty her reticule. 'I won this at the card tables. It's rather a lot of money, isn't it?'

'It is indeed.'

'And it's yours. Now if Brummell and his friends try to threaten you again, you'll have enough to move somewhere else where they can't harm you.'

'But this is yours. I can't take it.'

'You must and I don't want it.'

There was a harsh finality about her words which made Corry wince. It was clear that Crystal was suffering terribly, but he doubted whether it was due to her brief entry into the polite world. He had seen her earlier happiness and guessed that she had found a man to love. Now there was only abject misery in her.

'Aren't you going to tell me what is really wrong?' he asked gently.

Crystal put up barricades at once.

'I can't.'

'Please tell me if you need help. You're like a daughter to me and I don't like being shut out.'

'I'm sorry, but that's the way it has to be. I know that I owe you everything, but –'

'You owe me nothing. Whatever small assistance I gave you has been repaid a hundred-fold. And not simply because of your agreement to fit in with Dunstone's disgraceful plan, or by reason of this money you've won. Your life has been my reward. I thought you knew that.'

Drops of moisture hung on Crystal's downcast lashes, but she couldn't talk of Melfort, not even to Basil.

'I do know and I love you, Mr Corry. I'd like to explain things, but it's not possible. After this, I must leave London.'

'Yes, I suppose so. You might be recognised.'

'I'll have to think where to go.'

'Now there I might be of some use to you. I had a letter today from a Mrs Shuttle, sister of an old friend of mine who died recently. His name was Thomas Brett. It may provide the answer to your future. Give me a few days to get in touch with Mrs Shuttle. Tomorrow we'll find you some lodgings nearby. Then no one will know where you are. Please say yes.'

Crystal looked at Basil's anxious face and nodded.

'Thank you, I'll do as you suggest. I don't quite understand how Mrs Shuttle can help, but it would be useful to have some idea where I'm going and what I'm going to do. I wasn't thinking very clearly before. I just wanted to rush away.'

'I understand and now you must go to bed. It's late and you look exhausted. I'm not going to explain about Thomas and his sister just now as I don't want to raise any hopes which might later be dashed.'

'All right and I am tired.' Crystal hoped that Basil wouldn't guess the real cause of her fatigue and that she would be well away from London before her condition became obvious. 'Good night, Mr Corry.'

'Good night, my dear.'

Basil watched Crystal mount the stairs, his anger smouldering anew as he thought about Viscount Dunstone. Then his common sense returned. Whatever evil Somerset had done, he hadn't been responsible for Crystal's present pit of despair. Only the man she loved could have drained all the happiness and life out of her.

He, Corry, would probably never learn who the culprit was. Crystal was too loyal, too brave, to give him away and Basil swore softly as he picked up a candlestick and made his way to his room.

'I hope you rot in hell, whoever you are,' he said as he put the flickering light beside his bed. 'You've broken my girl's heart. You deserve to die for that, damn you. You deserve to die.'

The next day Fanny packed a basket with food prepared by Mrs Moloney and went to Hampstead to meet Peter.

Since Rupert Somerset had raped her, she had lived in mortal dread that Heslop would discover the truth. Often she caught him looking at her in perturbation, but so far she had managed to convince him that nothing was wrong.

They sat together on the grass, their eyes screwed up against the sun, an uneasiness lying between them.

'Thanks for the food, Fan,' said, Peter. 'I 'ope it don't leave you short.'

She gave a laugh which didn't sound quite right.

'What, in Winnie's kitchen? Don't worry yerself about that. Plenty more where that came from.'

'All right, I won't worry about the food. I'll worry about you instead.'

'Me?' She braced herself for another spell of evasions and lies. 'What are you worryin' about me for? I'm as bright as a new pin.'

'I don't reckon you are. There's summat different about you. 'As been for some weeks now. Wish you'd tell me what's amiss.'

'If there were anythin', you'd be the first to know,' said Fanny with determined cheerfulness. 'What a fretter you are.'

'You've lost weight.'

'Oh come on! I'm as plump as a Christmas goose.'

'No, yer not. Think I'm blind, do yer? Any road, I can feel what's not there, can't I?'

'What rubbish you do talk, Peter Heslop.'

'It ain't rubbish.'

Fanny could see he was like a dog with a bone, not to be put off.

'Well, if you must know, it's a bit of woman's trouble. You've got a mother and sisters, so you knows what I mean. Now stop askin' me daft questions and embarrassin' me. Let's talk about our 'ouse what we're goin' to 'ave one day.'

Peter lay back, only half satisfied. Perhaps it was just woman's trouble, as Fan claimed. Then again, perhaps it was something else. Whatever the truth of it, she wasn't going to speak of it that afternoon and so he gave up.

'All right, if yer likes. What about the bedroom?'

'Sauce-box.' Fanny gave a quick sigh of relief. 'What about it?'

'I'll 'ave it painted all black unless yer give us a kiss 'ere and now.'

Fanny leaned over, feeling the heat of Heslop's body

through her thin dress. It took every ounce of courage in her not to flinch at his closeness, for it reminded her of another man who had pressed himself against her, laughing as he had robbed her of what should have been Peter's.

'That's better,' said Heslop with a grin. 'Nothin' like a smacker to git the conversation goin'. Now, me girl; what colour 'ud you like our bedroom to be?'

Charlotte's relief when she heard that Louis-Rey was home was unbounded.

She sent Florrie to him with a message to meet her that afternoon at their favourite rendezvous. It was a tiny farm which lay behind the bustle of fashionable Piccadilly; a Petit Trianon or world in miniature. The farm was looked after by a Mrs Searle, who had been put in charge of it by the king. She wore a hooped skirt and tall headdress, some thirty odd years out of date, milking the cows and welcoming her visitors with a sunny smile and a glass of syllabub. She had a soft heart for lovers and never sought to discover what was going on behind the barn where a wooden bench had been set under the trees.

'You don't know how glad I am to see you, darling,' said Charlotte, when she and Louis-Rey had paid their respects to Mrs Searle, leaving Florrie to help with the milking. 'And it's not just because I love you so much. My mind is in such a turmoil I don't know where to turn.'

'Quietly, sweetheart, quietly.' Louis-Rey saw the genuine distress in Charlotte, quick to console her. 'First give me a kiss and then tell me what's happened to upset you so.'

Charlotte searched every line of John's face, now so dear to her. Harsh, perhaps, yet it was strong and full of character, the eyes straight and true.

Willingly, Charlotte raised her head, soothed by the feel

of his lips against her own, glad of his arms about her. When he let her go she sighed deeply.

'I don't know where to begin. I'm not really sure of my facts, but I have to unburden myself or I shall go mad.'

'Surely it's not as bad as that?'

'I pray it isn't, but I'm not certain.'

'Well, tell me the situation as you see it and perhaps between us we can decide on the right course to take.'

'You're so sensible, John.'

'That sounds rather dull.'

'Not to me as I feel at present. You see, it began when Rupert asked me to help him with a wager he'd made.'

Louis-Rey listened in growing anger. He didn't like Dunstone and the unhappiness he had caused his sister did nothing to lessen John's poor opinion of him.

'And though I'm breaking my promise to Rupert,' Charlotte ended, 'you're so much a part of me that I can't keep things from you.'

'Of course you can't, but so far nothing you have said matches the pain in your eyes, ill-begotten though your brother's actions were.'

'That's because I haven't told it all yet. John, I think there was more to that bet than Rupert led me to believe. He was so insistent that I gave my oath not to mention it to anyone. Naturally, I thought at the time that was simply because if anyone found out before the two weeks were up, Rupert would lose the wager and have to pay a large sum of money which he didn't have.

'At first I didn't want to do it. Then, because you were away and I was missing you so, I thought it might be rather fun. Now, looking back, I don't think I really considered the matter properly. John, I believe there was something really bad behind it all. Crystal was so cold and distant when we first met. Rupert assured me that she had agreed to help him; now I'm not sure that she did. After a while she thawed to me; perhaps she realised that I didn't know what Rupert had done.'

'But what could he have done to force her?'

'I don't know, but I'm going to find out. Then, when I saw Stuart and heard what he had to say, I felt worse than ever.'

Louis-Rey held Charlotte's hand whilst she told him about the earl's relationship with Crystal Yorke, human enough to feel a spasm of relief when he learned that Melfort had released Charlotte.

'What must I do, John?'

'Ask Crystal to come and see you,' he returned promptly. 'Get her to tell you exactly what happened. Then we'll consider our next move.'

'Of course, that is the obvious thing to do. Oh, my love, I'm so glad you're with me again.'

'So am I.' Louis-Rey dismissed Somerset from his mind as he drank deep of Charlotte's beauty. 'Now, since you've made a clean breast of things, do you think I might have another kiss? Dearest Charlotte, I missed you, too, you know.'

Charlotte did not have to go looking for Crystal. The evening after John's return Crystal called upon Charlotte to return a pearl necklace which she had been wearing on the last night of the bet.

'I'm sorry I didn't give it back to you at once. I put it in my reticule and have only just discovered it.'

'It doesn't matter in the least.'

Charlotte's heart sank as she watched Crystal's face. It was as cold and hostile as it had been on the first occasion they had met. The friendship and affection built up between them had vanished completely. It wasn't going to be easy to question Crystal in her present mood.

But Charlotte didn't shirk her task. Louis-Rey had given her the courage to tackle the unpleasant job and she got down to business at once, wasting no time on preliminaries.

'I understand you were Stuart's mistress,' she said when she had sent Florrie from the room. 'I didn't know that when I agreed to help my brother with that prank.'

'Prank!' Crystal was very pale but in absolute control of herself. 'You put too light a name to what he did.'

'What exactly did he do?' Charlotte met Crystal's eyes unflinchingly. 'You see, I don't think I really know.'

'Then I will tell you, Lady Charlotte, since it doesn't matter any more. Your brother threatened to ruin Mr Corry if we didn't agree to my taking part in his scheme on which so much money rode. He and his friend, Brummell, would have put Mr Corry out of business.'

'Mr Corry? Brummell?' Charlotte was very still, feeling as though a storm was about to break. 'I don't understand. Who is Mr Corry and what did the Beau have to do with all this? You must explain more clearly.'

'With pleasure.'

Crystal didn't know how she managed to keep upright in her chair. Waves of sickness assaulted her and she felt lost without the strength of Stuart's love. Corry had found her comfortable lodgings quite near to Swan Street, but it was lonely there without him, Winnie, Fanny and Benjamin. She could see the concern and doubt in Charlotte, but this time she didn't soften towards her. Charlotte had been part of it all and Crystal was not in a forgiving frame of mind.

When she had finished telling the whole story, Charlotte said faintly:

'Oh, my God!'

'Yes, I prayed to God, too, but He didn't listen. The earl thinks I did it to get myself a rich husband because I could never be his wife. That role will be yours.'

'No.' Charlotte was trying to come to terms with the ugly truth. 'No, Stuart and I are not going to marry. I'm in love with another man and the earl has released me.'

'It makes no difference.' Crystal was looking down at her hands. 'His lordship has well and truly sent me packing and I'm not sorry. What sport you've made of me. Used as a pawn in a bet; the earl taking me to bed because I was a woman of no account whose name didn't have to be protected. It was safe enough for him to tumble me in the blankets. He's like the rest of you; shallow, selfish, cruel and with no thought for others.'

'No! You're wrong. Stuart isn't a bit like that. I'm sure he wouldn't –'

'But I know he did. Your brother got his money, you enjoyed a laugh at my expense, the earl had some cheap satisfaction. All I got was a broken heart. No, that's not quite true. I got one other thing; Melfort's seed. Yes, Lady Charlotte, I'm going to have the earl's child. Isn't that the perfect end to a story such as mine?'

Charlotte couldn't move as Crystal almost ran from the room. Her limbs felt leaden, her brain equally numb. When Florrie returned a few moments later with a freshly ironed gown, Charlotte stirred at last. Her maid exclaimed at her mistress's pallor, but Charlotte silenced her with a motion of her hand.

'Don't fuss, Florrie, I'm not the one who needs your pity. I'm going to write a note to Mr Louis-Rey and you are to take it to him immediately.

'Oh, that poor, poor girl! What have we all done to her?'

Seven

Charlotte's meeting with Louis-Rey took place in her parents' house just off Grosvenor Square.

This was no time for the pretence of the toy farm, and neither could Charlotte risk seeing John alone at that late hour. Thus when the door opened to admit him to the magnificence of the Earl of Selkirk's residence, he was escorted by a liveried flunkey to the second floor where Annabel Malvern, Duchess of Baverstock sat by the window, Charlotte by her side.

The duchess was of a great age, wizened by time, but not in the least put out by it. She wore a fashionable gown, a wig dressed with pearls and rubies, her gnarled hands glittering with rings.

'Thank you for coming.' Charlotte went forward to greet John. 'I'm sorry we have to talk here, but I'm sure you understand the reason.'

'Of course I do. I would never put your reputation at risk.'

'Dear John. Come and meet the duchess. You needn't worry about her. She's deaf and won't hear a thing we say. Aunt Belle, this is Mr Louis-Rey.'

The duchess's alert blue eyes sized John up in a trice, her ear-trumpet raised as if to catch the introduction.

'Eh? What's that, girl? Speak up for heaven's sake. All

you young people mumble today. Don't know what's the matter with you. You've got tongues in your heads so why don't you use 'em? What d'yer say your beau's name is?'

Charlotte gave Annabel a suspicious look, mouthing her words carefully.

'I didn't say he was my beau.'

'Didn't have to, you foolish chit. Lurray, was it?'

'No, dear; Louis-Rey. I have to speak to him about something very important, but of course I can't see him alone. Usually Florrie's been with me – more or less – but it's her free evening. You don't mind, do you? I must talk with him.'

'Walk with him? Well, you won't get much exercise in here. Still, if it's what you want to do you won't worry me. Minnie.' The duchess turned to her elderly maid who was casting her eyes to heaven. 'Be off with you. Lady Charlotte wants to take a stroll with her young man and they don't want you hanging about.'

'You see, it's hopeless,' said Charlotte with a faint grimace, 'But she's a dear, really. We can be quite open, for Her Grace won't understand us.'

Quickly, Charlotte outlined her meeting with Crystal, very near to tears when she had finished.

Louis-Rey was as shocked as Charlotte had been. He had not expected that Dunstone would stoop to such depths.

'He's my brother,' Charlotte went on, her voice unsteady, 'but I hate him now. And I don't understand how Brummell could have lent himself to use blackmail on an innocent shopkeeper.'

'We're not sure that he did.'

'But Crystal said that Rupert went to speak to the Beau in the shop and the Beau supported him.'

'We've only got the viscount's word for that.' John was grim. 'Forgive me, my dear, but to me your brother's word is suspect. I don't know Brummell, but from what I've seen and heard of him I cannot believe he would act in such a way. How do we know exactly what your brother said to Brummell or Brummell to him?'

Charlotte paused to consider that possibility.

'No, I suppose you're right. I hadn't thought of that. What am I to do? Stuart has washed his hands of Crystal Yorke because of that absurd wager, and she is bearing his child.'

'The answer to that is clear. You must see the earl and tell him the whole truth, promise or no promise to your brother. You cannot be a party to this sordid mess. Tell Stuart everything and let him take care of the situation.'

'Quite right, John Louis-Rey. Very sound advice.'

John and Charlotte turned in blank amazement to stare at the duchess who had laid aside her hearing-aid and was helping herself to a pinch of snuff.

'Aunt Belle! You heard what we said.'

'Of course I did, you nincompoop.'

'But you're deaf.'

'Only when I want to be.'

'But my conversation with John was private.'

'So it should be if that abominable reptile Dunstone is involved. I can remember every single thing he's said to my face because, like you, he thought I was deaf. That's why I've cut him out of my Will.'

'I don't know what to say.'

'Your betrothed has just told you what to say and do. You are to be married, I trust?'

'Definitely.'

'I'm not sure, Your Grace.'

The duchess put her head on one side.

'Why aren't you sure? Don't you love the gel enough to make her your wife?'

'I worship her,' replied John quietly. 'She is the breath of life to me and I don't know how I will exist without her.'

'John –'

'Be quiet, Charlotte, you've had your say.'

'But John thinks he's not good enough for me.'

'That true, young man?'

'It is patently the case, Your Grace. I am comfortably placed, but not rich. My family is of good stock, but not of the aristocracy.'

'What twaddle!'

'The Earl and Countess of Selkirk may not think so.'

'Don't take any notice of Daphne; she's a featherhead. Talk to Marcus. My guess is that all he wants is for Charlotte to be happy. They'll be home in a couple of days, so you'll soon find out that I'm right. And you, you simpleton. Go and see Stuart and make your confession. If I were Melfort I'd give you a damned good hiding for your mischief, but I daresay he's too soft for that.'

Charlotte went and knelt by Annabel's chair.

'You won't say anything about this, will you? Not even to Minnie.'

'Of course I shan't speak of it. You may be a cretin, but I'm not, and I certainly won't mention a word of it to Minnie Harper. It would get her far too excited and she's silly enough as it is. I'm going to have a sleep. Go and sit at the far end of the room, the pair of you. I shan't see you and everyone knows I'm as deaf as a post, so I shan't hear you either.'

As Louis-Rey bent to kiss Her Grace's hand she gave him a saucy wink.

'I like you, m'boy. Not a pretty face, but an interesting one. Charlotte's had too much of her own way until now and needs a firm hand. I suspect you've got one. Good luck to you and remember. Ignore Daphne. She's a bigger fool than Minnie.'

Somewhat dazed, John and Charlotte sat together on the window-seat overlooking well tended rosebeds.

'I had no idea.' Charlotte was apologetic. 'I really did think she was deaf. Are you very angry with me?'

Louis-Rey chuckled.

'For introducing me to the most fascinating *grande dame* I've ever met? Certainly not. I think the duchess is quite delightful. If I weren't hopelessly in love with you, I think I'd offer for her. Do you think she'd have me?'

Charlotte relaxed as she laid her head against John's shoulder.

'I'm sure she would; how could she resist you? But she's not going to get the chance. You belong to me, and don't you ever forget it.'

When Charlotte found that the Earl of Melfort had gone away for two weeks, travelling in the South and West, her heart sank.

She had braced herself to face Stuart, only to discover that there was no way of reaching him and the weight on her conscience grew heavier and heavier. John comforted her and counselled patience. So did the Duchess upon being told of Stuart's departure.

'Well, you'll have to wait until he gets back, won't you?'

'If only he wasn't moving about I could write to him.'

'But he is moving about and what you've got to tell him is better said to his face.'

'But, Aunt Belle, what about Crystal?'

'Mm, hard on her, I agree. Still, Melfort's the only one who can remedy her plight.'

'I suppose so.'

'I know so and you'd better think what you're going to say to your mother and father when they get back tomorrow.'

'I'm determined to marry John.'

Annabel cackled.

'I know, but you're not looking forward to your mother's hysterics, are you? Ah well. Everything worth while has its price.'

And Daphne Somerset did have hysterics on the following day when Charlotte badly announced her plans.

'Charlotte! Are you mad? Who is this man, Louis-Rey? I've never heard of him.'

'You have now, mother, and I love him.'

'But what about Melfort?'

'I've just explained that to you. Stuart has agreed to let me go. After all, he hadn't actually asked for my hand, had he?'

'No, but it was clear that he was going to do so. Marcus, speak to the girl. She is quite out of her mind. A penniless nobody instead of the son of a marquis and an extremely rich one at that.'

The small party had gathered in the duchess's room, the countess blissfully ignorant that Annabel was drinking in every word and laughing inwardly.

Marcus regarded his daughter speculatively. Most of his contemporaries considered him to be a decent, sensible sort of man, not overburned by brains, but sound by reason of birth and breeding. But Selkirk was much more intelligent and perceptive than they gave him credit for. It had been obvious to him from the moment of his return that something was wrong with Charlotte. Having listened to her tale, he was equally certain that whatever it was had nothing to do with Stuart Haversham or Louis-Rey.

Like the marquis, he'd often wondered whether the match between Charlotte and Stuart would ever come to anything. Devised by their respective mothers, there was always a strong possibility that it would founder on the rocks of another relationship.

'You really love this man, Charlie?' he asked finally. 'Not just a passing thing, is it?'

'No, father it's not. My love for John is true and forever. I want him for my husband.'

The countess let out a shriek.

'You are insane! One day you could be a marchioness.'

'Yes, I could be a desolate, unhappy marchioness, or I can be the wife of John and the happiest woman on earth.'

'Well, that's something to think about, Daphne.'

'Be quiet, Marcus! Charlotte, don't listen to your father. He's so weak that he'd let you marry a blacksmith if you wanted to. You say yourself this man has no money. What are you going to live on?'

'He has some and then there's what my godmother left me.'

'That won't be enough to keep you in handkerchiefs.'

'But what I'm going to leave Charlie will be. They tell me I'm the third richest women in England, although how they know that I can't imagine. It'll all be hers when I'm gone.'

Daphne's stupefaction was as great as John's and Charlotte's had been earlier, but Marcus merely grinned at Annabel.

'Wondered when you'd start interfering.'

'But – but you're deaf!'

The duchess gave Daphne a pitying look.

'And you're brainless.'

'How dare you! Marcus, did you hear what she said to me? And did you know she could hear?'

'Of course he knew. Do stop prattling woman. Marcus?'

The earl pursed his lips.

'Met this man have you, Annabel?'

'Yes.'

'What did you think of him?'

'I liked him. Good type; right for Charlie.'

'That'll do for me. Daphne, for pity's sake be quiet. You must have known making plans for Charlotte to marry when she was still in her cradle wasn't sensible. She's in love, aren't you, my dear?'

'Very much, father.'

'I'll have to see him, of course, but if Annabel approves I've no doubt that I shall, too.'

'Dear father; thank you.'

Whilst the duchess gave instructions to Minnie to escort the lachrymose countess to her own room, Selkirk turned to Charlotte.

'There's something else bothering you, isn't there? What is it?'

Charlotte couldn't meet the earl's eyes.

'I can't tell you. I'm sorry, but it's a matter you'll have to find out about from someone other than me. All I can say is that it has nothing to do with John and me and thank you again for saying I can have him.'

Later, after Marcus had quietened his wife, he said meditatively:

'I don't like what I see in Charlotte.'

'Neither do I.' Daphne was still tearful and highly indignant to discover how completely Annabel had fooled her. 'But you agreed, although it's the most ridiculous thing I've ever heard of.'

'I'm not talking about Louis-Rey,' returned the earl with some impatience. 'If you hadn't been so busy screeching at the girl, you'd have seen there was both worry and sadness in her.'

'I should think so. After all –'

Marcus moved to the window, giving up any hope of getting his wife to understand what he was talking about. His brows met as he felt the gnawing anxiety in him increase. What was it that Charlotte couldn't tell him, when they had always been so close?

Then the answer came to him, creeping into his mind with unpleasant certainty. Rupert had been a great disappointment to him. Like everyone else he was aware of the viscount's behaviour and it hurt. Being a wild young buck was one thing; being a blackguard was quite different.

Charlotte wouldn't talk about her brother whatever he had done, but another question had taken the place of the first and the earl's eyes were hard as he turned to look back at his weeping wife.

Just what had Dunstone done to make Charlotte look as she did and, more important, how was he, Selkirk, going to find out about it?

Ten days after the strange disappearance of Lady Jane Markham which had set so many tongues wagging, Fanny Bethall's world came to an end.

Peter's suspicions had been lulled only temporarily by her talk of women's troubles and he soon began his questioning again.

'You ain't the same and it's not good tellin' me you are. I'm not a thickhead, even though some might say I was. Now, come on, Fan, out with it.'

Fanny was tired and unhappy. Crystal had told her all about the viscount and his threats and she had missed her friend during the three weeks the latter was playing the fine lady. She had also learned that Crystal had lost the man she loved, although Crystal wouldn't give his name.

'Don't go on and on so. Give us a bit o' peace, do.'

'No, I won't, not until yer gives us the truth.'

'All right, all right!' Fanny reached the end of her tether and exploded. 'You wants the truth, Peter Heslop, so you can 'ave it. You won't believe me, I knows it, but 'ere it is for what it's worth.'

Heslop listened, his facing growing thunderous.

'You 'spect me to believe that?'

'No, I just said you wouldn't, not a moment ago. But it's what 'appened. I were molested and I couldn't save meself. 'E were strong and there were two others besides.'

''Oo was 'e? I want 'is name.'

By now Fanny's anger was spent and she saw at once the risk of giving Peter Viscount Dunstone's name.

'We wasn't introduced,' she said shortly. ''E just raped me, is all.'

'I think you're lyin' again. You do know 'oo it were.'

'Well, if that's what you thinks of me you'd best be gone, 'adn't you?'

'Reckon I 'ad, you rotten whore. I asked you times enough to – to – well – you know. But no, I weren't good enough, I suppose. You wanted some fancy gentleman to give your favours to. I 'ope 'e paid yer well.'

''E paid me nowt. Now be off with you.'

'Don't worry, I'm goin' and I don't want to see you no more. I thought so much of you and all the time you were a Jezebel. Well, I've learned me lesson and good riddance to you.'

Peter went running down the grassy slope, whilst Fanny's eyes filled with tears.

She was still crying when she reached the lodgings which Corry had taken for Crystal, finding the latter packing her boxes while Basil watched.

'Let us come with you, Crystal,' said Fanny blowing her nose and trying to regain her composure. 'Peter made me tell 'im about that night. I've 'eld out against 'im for so long, but 'e were that scratchy today I gave up. 'E didn't think I were tellin' the truth; I knew 'e wouldn't. Now 'e never wants to see me again. I can't stay 'ere, Mr Corry, truly I can't.'

'My dear Fanny, I'm so very sorry.' Basil rose and patted the maid's arm. 'If he's so blind about your character, perhaps you're better off without him. It's up to Crystal as to whether she wants company, but it might be good for her as well as for you.

'I've been telling her that I've heard from Mrs Shuttle, sister of a friend of mine recently deceased. He had a small shop with living quarters over it and Mrs Shuttle wants to sell it. It's in Bristol, a very pleasant place, and far enough away from London to be safe.'

Fanny turned to Crystal beseechingly.

'Let us come with you. I'll do anything. I'll work till I drop and I won't want no wages. Just a slip o' somewhere to sleep and a bite to eat, is all.'

'Dear Fanny, of course you can come, that is, if I'm going to Bristol. I still have to talk to Mr Corry about the cost of it all. I'll let you know in half an hour or so if it's going to be a possibility.'

'Thank you!' Fanny clasped her hands over Crystal's. 'Thank you for saying I can come. I'm sure summat can be worked out, don't you think, sir?'

'I wouldn't be surprised. Now run along, there's a good girl. Crystal and I have much to discuss.'

'I haven't any money to buy a shop,' said Crystal when Fanny had gone. 'I expect it's terribly expensive.'

'Not in the least. Thomas was ill for some time before he died. The place had got very run down. Mrs Shuttle and I have been extremely busy in the last few days. Letters by every coach going west and east, one might say. I've already acquired the premises and I used the money you won that night when you went gambling.'

'You've bought it already?' Crystal sat down abruptly. 'You mean it's yours now?'

'No, my dear girl, it's yours. It, and its contents, are in

your name. By the way, did I tell you it was a shop which sold snuff? You'll need something more to refurbish the place and get new stocks. You have the money I've saved from the sale of your boxes. Quite a nice little nest-egg. You have plenty of materials left to go on with your work and you can sell those along with the snuff. I'm going to give you a few really good silver boxes to attract your first customers.'

'I can't take your snuff-boxes.' Crystal held up a hand in protest. 'I feel bad enough that you have used money I wanted you to have to buy the shop.'

'Ah, but I always meant you to have it and I'm used to getting my own way.' Basil was unfolding a piece of dark blue velvet. 'Now, what do you think of this half-dozen?'

At the sight of them Crystal began to weep.

'It is too much; too generous.'

'How absurd you are and you'll make your eyes red if you carry on like that. Besides, these are not of undue value.'

'I don't know how to thank you. Ever since I took refuge in your area you've cared for me. And now this.'

'I've enjoyed every minute you've been with me, so be done with your arguments and your gratitude. I'm the one who should be grateful.'

'If I go –'

'When you go –'

'Promise me faithfully that you will never tell anyone where I am. Not anyone at all.'

Basil considered Crystal sombrely.

'Are you sure?'

'I'm very sure.'

'No hope of a reconciliation?'

'None whatsoever.'

'I'm sorry. I understand that you fainted yesterday and I couldn't help hearing you this morning.'

'I guessed you'd find out. I'd hoped to keep it from you so

that you wouldn't worry, but being sick is such a noisy thing, isn't it?'

'My dearest girl, I wish I could do more. You may stay here where I can look after you if you want to.'

'No, that wouldn't be a good idea, but I do thank you for the offer. It means a lot to me. The shop is ideal as a solution to my problems and I'm grateful to you for that as well.'

'Then it's all settled. You'll go tomorrow with Fanny. I've made all the arrangements and Mrs Shuttle will be waiting for you. Here's the address of the shop and the money I spoke of. Take good care of it, for you'll need it until you get established.'

Crystal took the purse and leaned to kiss Basil on the cheek.

'I'll write to you.'

'I shall expect you to.' Basil cleared his throat, his eyes misty. 'I'll miss you, Crystal.'

'And I you. Part of me wants to stay, but I know it wouldn't be right.'

'No, I don't suppose it would. Well, it's no good crying over spilt milk and I shall be weeping like Fanny before I know it. Come along, my dear, we both need to be survivors now. Let's go and ask Winnie to make us a nice cup of tea to help us on our way.'

Crystal and Fanny craned their necks to see all they could of the countryside around Bristol which was to be their new home. Standing at the confluence of the Rivers Avon and Frome, its charm was enhanced by the Clifton and Durdham Downs and the beauty of the Avon Gorge.

It was only when they alighted in the centre of the city that they realised how crowded a place it was. It had very narrow streets, some of the older houses so close together at the upper storeys that neighbours could almost lean out and shake hands.

The snuff shop was in the ancient thoroughfare of Christmas Steps, a place full of small shops with bow windows, hanging signs, and an air of eternity about it.

Mrs Shuttle was a well-rounded woman in her fifties, dressed in her best for the occasion. She wore a cambric frock buttoned behind, her shoulders covered by a Spanish vest. Her straw bonnet was profusely trimmed with ribbons, the outfit completed by York Tan gloves and leather slippers.

She gave Crystal an approving look as the driver and Fanny got the boxes from the roof of the coach.

'Yes, yes, you'll do very well,' she said as she unlocked the shop door. 'Not usual for a gel of your years to be selling snuff. Not usual for a woman of any age to do so, come to that. Still, as I always say to my husband, anything a man can do a woman can do better, for we've got more sense in our heads than they have. Now, let's light a few candles. I've had part of the shutters removed, but thought it safest to leave the rest.'

Crystal hardly heard Mrs Shuttle. The outside of the shop, with its leaded light windows and decorated fanlight, had been elegant enough, in spite of its air of decay.

Inside, the lure was more potent still. On one side there was a long mahogany counter, thickly coated with dust, on which stood brass scales, a further pair suspended from the beam across the ceiling. Behind the counter, the wall had been shelved completely and there were glass and earthenware storage jars so closely crammed together that they appeared to be jostling for space.

On the other side was another counter and a desk, where customers paid for their goods, with more jars on the floor gathering cobwebs.

'Thomas didn't have any help,' said Mrs Shuttle, holding a candestick aloft. 'He wasn't very good at cleaning either, but you can see that for yourself. Never mind, that's a nice strong maid you've brought with you and you won't find it difficult to get extra scrubbing women to put the place to rights.'

'I expect we'll manage.' Crystal had moved behind the main counter, her own flame flickering over the labels written in a cramped hand. 'What a lot of different snuffs. I'd no idea there were so many. And what wonderful names some of them have. Do you know what sort of snuff each one is, Mrs Shuttle?'

'Drat this place. I can't see a hand in front of me. Ah, girl, you're just in time; you, too, coachman. Help me get more of these boards down so we're not bumping about in the dark.'

The driver muttered a protest, but Mrs Shuttle silenced him with a few coins and soon the shop opened up like a flower whose petals had been touched by the first light of morning.

Crystal gazed round in delight. It was incredibly dirty and the shelves were worn thin at the edges where the containers had been pulled back and forth for many years. But it was hers and she knew what she could make of it. The snuff jars, suitably dealt with, would remain where they were. On the other side would be the boxes, carefully laid out on velvet like Basil's had been placed.

'That's better.' Mrs Shuttle dusted her gloves, tutting in annoyance. 'Really, Thomas was most neglectful. I wonder anyone ever came inside, for they would surely leave it like chimney sweeps. Now, you were asking me if I knew anything about the snuffs. I have some knowledge because my father was very partial to it. Let me see.' She peered short-sightedly at the faded labels. 'What an atrocious hand my brother had. You'll have to write all these anew. Yes, Seville. That's light brown, as you see, finely ground and perfumed with orange. Prince's Special is black, moist and coarse-ground, but one adds a finer-milled variety to temper it. It's scented with Otto of Roses.

'Macouba – that comes from Martinique, and High Dry Toast is exceptionally finely ground with a nutty flavour. Irish in origin, I believe.'

'How clever you are. I'm sure I'll never get to remember them all. There's one here called Bureau and another named Bordeaux.'

'Bureau's very old. The Cavaliers used it. Made up of about six different snuffs, so Thomas once told me. Bordeaux's a medium-ground mixture, very scented; a blend of moist and dry snuffs. That's about all I know, but there's a book in the cupboard over there with all of them listed and explaining their colour, texture, and perfume. Thomas may have been untidy but he was very careful about his snuffs.'

'You have been so kind, Mrs Shuttle. I'm most grateful to you for the time you've spared.'

'Tush, it was nothing. Now, here are the keys and the deeds of the place. That door leads through to a kitchen and an outhouse. Upstairs there are two bedrooms and a box-room, although goodness knows what condition they are in. Quite dreadful, I expect.'

After Mrs Shuttle had been escorted to her carriage, Crystal and Fanny explored. As Thomas's sister had warned them, the top part of the premises was every bit as bad as the shop itself. Up the narrow, twisting stairs they found only one room with a bed in it. The other two had been used to dump empty cannisters or boxes in which supplies had come.

'Oh dear,' said Crystal when they returned to the

kitchen. 'There's an awful lot to do, isn't there? We need buckets and brushes and –'

'I'll see to it.' Fanny was coaxing the old black stove to light. 'Seein' 'ow you are, you can't do much.'

Fanny had been aware of Crystal's condition almost before the latter had known it herself, and was determined that her friend should do no more than a little light dusting.

'Tomorrow we'll find a couple of women to help you.' Crystal was feeling sick again but trying not to shew it and worry Fanny. 'We'll get a man to clear away all the old furniture and rubbish and after everything's clean we'll get new beds, table and chairs and whatever else we need.'

'Goin' to cost a bit.'

'I know, but Mr Corry's been terribly generous. I think he must have known his friend Thomas very well and guessed we'd have to replace everything.'

'You'd best buy a weddin' ring, too.'

Crystal watched the steam coming from the rusty kettle, puzzled by Fanny's suggestion.

'A wedding ring? What for?'

''Cos when the baby comes it 'as to 'ave a father, don't it?'

'But it won't have one.'

'No, but we can pretend it 'as.'

'I don't see –'

'You're a soldier's widow,' said Fanny, washing up two mugs in a pan of water she had got from the pump in the yard. 'Poor devil died afore 'e knew 'e were goin' to be a pa. Everyone'll feel sorry for you that way.'

'But it's so dishonest.'

'Lord, Crystal Yorke, ain't you got no sense in that pretty 'ead o' yours? 'Oo do you think is goin' to come buyin' snuff from an 'arlot? No, you've got to be respectable.'

'Respectable! That's the last thing I am.'

'Well, you'll 'ave to play-act it. 'Ere, try this. Looks a funny colour, but it's wet an' warm.'

'It's not too bad,' said Crystal, after a hesitant sip. 'But I saw a shop selling tea two doors away from here. That's something else we'll buy tomorrow, Fanny, and some decent china to drink it from. I do miss Winnie and Mr Corry, but suddenly I feel almost happy again. There's so much we've got to think about that neither of us will have time to brood.

'Dear Fanny, isn't it exciting? We're both going to begin all over again.'

Eight

Charlotte's interview with Stuart upon his return to London was every bit as bad as she had expected it to be.

John had wanted to accompany her, but she had refused.

'No, this is something I have to do myself. I know that Stuart will be furious and he has a right to be.'

'I don't want him ranting and raging at you.' Louis-Rey had been sharp. 'I won't permit him to do that.'

'You won't be able to stop him and I must do it alone.'

The earl listened to Charlotte with increasing anger, exploding in the wrath she had feared when she reached the end of her story.

'I know what wrong I have done Crystal and you, too, Stuart,' said Charlotte when the worst of the storm had died down. 'But I didn't know she was your mistress, nor had I any idea that Rupert and Brummell had coerced her. John isn't sure that Rupert is telling the truth when he said the Beau was part of all this; I'm not sure either.'

'I'll find out.' The earl was now in a much more frightening mood, cold, withdrawn, almost a stranger. 'I shall deal with Dunstone, too, but you are not without blame. You were always far too fond of playing tricks on people regardless of their feelings or their ability to stand up for themselves.'

'I know.' Charlotte didn't hang her head. She deserved

the punishment Stuart was administering and she knew it. 'I would give anything in the world to undo the harm, but it's too late. And now Crystal is pregnant by you.'

'The point hadn't escaped me.'

'I went to Mr Corry's shop yesterday, but he said Crystal had gone away and he had no idea of her destination. What will you do?'

'Find her, of course. I'm sure Corry knows more than he was willing to tell you.'

'She thought you were merely using her as a toy; that's my fault as well, because she thinks you are like Rupert and me. Stuart, I'm so desperately sorry. I would never knowingly do anything to hurt you or Crystal either. I realise that I've been a fool and worse, but —'

'— you're not like your brother. No, I know that.'

Melfort walked over to Charlotte and saw the unnatural brightness of her eyes.

'You're a thoughtless idiot, Charlie, but you're right. You wouldn't deliberately cause real pain.'

'Will you ever forgive me?'

'I expect so. I always do, don't I?'

When Charlotte had wept on Stuart's shoulder, vastly relieved by the comfort of his arms around her, she said miserably:

'I'm terrified that mother and father will find out about this. Mother can never see any wrong in Rupert. I suppose I've been just as bad as she in the past. But I'm not sure if father knows what sort of man he is.'

'Selkirk is a very shrewd judge of character. I'd be very surprised if he had any illusions about his son. Now I must go and talk to Brummell. Do you want me to take you home first?'

'No, no, Florrie is waiting for me in the hall. I hope you find Crystal.'

'So do I, although God knows what she will say to me if I do. No, don't start crying again, Charlie. Not all the fault is yours and Rupert's. I leapt to the wrong conclusion and gave Crystal no chance to explain. She said if I loved her I would trust her, but I demanded reasons.'

'She couldn't explain. Rupert had forced her to silence.'

'Rupert had forced her to many things and I'll make him pay for it. But if Crystal refuses to have anything more to do with me, it will be no more than justice.'

When the earl had seen Charlotte safely on her way he went to No. 4, Chesterfield Street, the small Mayfair home of George Brummell.

He found the Beau engaged in tying one of his exquisite cravats, a swathe of starched muslin wound meticulously round the neck, creased at the front by a series of downward motions of the chin. As usual, Brummell was holding court whilst dressing. Prince Esterhazy and Lords Yarmouth, Cholmondeley, Fife and Petersham were discussing bloodstock, the latest lover of the Marchioness of Everley, and the perfect cut of the Beau's coat.

For a moment Stuart watched Brummell, wondering as Basil Corry had once done exactly how this elegant young man had become not only a leader of the polite world, but a suave tyrant whom even the greatest in the land feared to offend.

Brummell was of good middle-stock origin, his father once Secretary to Lord North, the Prime Minister. After Eton and Oriel, the Beau had been honoured by the Prince of Wales with a cornetcy in his own regiment, the Tenth Hussars. Tiring of military discipline, such as it was in that regiment, Brummell resigned his commission and set out to conquer London early in 1798.

Under the patronage of the Prince and the beautiful Duchess of Devonshire, George's rise had been meteoric.

Yet powerful friends alone couldn't have made this demi-god.

The earl studied the Beau's face, rather long and neither plain nor handsome. His complexion was fair, his hair light brown. The grey eyes were steady under eyebrows which he used as weapons against those who bored or offended him.

No one who was anyone would order goods from a tradesman without consulting Brummell first. Every fête, ball, drum or levée called for Mr Brummell's advice before a hostess could be sure that she would have a success.

Stuart finished his survey, no wiser than before. For all his self-assurance, wit, stern rule, and charm, Brummell wouldn't have reached such a peak amongst the nobility had he been a mere mountebank. Society, proud and very aware of its own importance, would have soon sent a pretender packing.

The Beau looked up from his task and inclined his head.

'Melfort; a good morning to you. Have you come for a lesson in the fine art of arranging a cravat?'

'No, I've come to talk to you and in private, if you please.'

The grey eyes wandered over the earl pensively. Brummell had heard a note in Stuart's voice which was foreign to him and was intrigued. Furthermore, despite his somewhat blasé greeting, Brummell rather liked Stuart. He turned to the voluble group behind him, silencing it with a single glance.

'Gentlemen, you will have to excuse me. I have business to discuss with Melfort. Robinson will give you some excellent Madeira, and I won't be long.'

While Robinson, the Beau's valet who was almost as famous as his master, attended to his guests, George led the way to a small library where he had an enviable collection of books and some fine pieces of porcelain displayed to best advantage.

'Well, m'dear Stuart, what is amiss with you? I swear you look as if you're about to challenge someone to a duel.'

'I probably am.'

'Good God, how exhausting. Why do you come to me? Do you want my advice on how to hold a pistol?'

'I know how to hold a pistol – far better than you do.'

'Then why –?' The Beau's eyebrows elevated a fraction. 'I hope I am wrong in supposing that I am your quarry.'

'I'm not sure whether you are or not.'

Brummel sighed and sat down.

'Stuart, riddles are well enough in their place, but I have neither the time nor inclination for them just now. Why exactly have you come to see me and what is wrong with you?'

'You want the plain, unvarnished truth, or shall I wrap it up for you?'

'Pray don't put yourself to such trouble. The blunt truth will do.'

When the earl had finished, Brummell said quietly:

'You thought that of me?'

'No. No, not really. George, I'm sorry, but I'm utterly distracted. I've behaved abominably and treated the woman I love disgracefully and now she's going to have my child and I haven't the faintest idea where she is.'

'In view of the circumstances,' said Brummell, rising to pour brandy into two glasses, 'I shall grant you pardon because it is clear that you're quite out of your mind. Here, drink this. It'll do you more good than Madeira. Let me see – Dunstone.'

The Beau was silent for a moment, then he nodded.

'Yes, I did see Rupert Somerset in Corry's shop not so long ago. He came and asked me whether he should buy a gold or silver box for his mother. Out of the depths of my great love for mankind I advised him what to do. And that is all we spoke of.'

'Forgive me.'

'I've already done so, as I've just said. You're not responsible for what you're saying or doing. But, Stuart, let me give you a piece of advice and it'll be more useful than that which I gave to Dunstone.

'Be careful when you deal with Rupert Somerset. He is a worthless viper, but he's also a dangerous one. Wear gloves when you handle him. And now I must return to those waiting to hang upon my every word concerning the relative excellence of Bath coating and superfine.'

Melfort gave a reluctant laugh.

'Sometimes, George, I think you're nothing but a damned clever fraud.'

'Ah, but you'll never be certain about that will you, m'dear fellow? Neither will anyone else. That's the knack, don't you see? That's the knack.' Then the amusement left Brummell's eyes and they were as cold and remorseless as a winter's sea. 'When you see Dunstone, tell him something from me, will you? I do not permit my name to be used in such a grossly outrageous fashion. Tell him also that if you don't finish him off, I will. On second thoughts, I don't think I shall wait for you. As far as his world is concerned, Rupert Somerset is already dead.'

There was a moon on the night when Viscount Dunstone left Brooke's in the company of Percy Sheffield.

They strolled along for a while, laughing mockingly at the foibles of those with whom they had been playing cards. They didn't notice how far they had gone, startled when a figure stepped out in front of them, barring their passage.

'Lord Percy, I would advise you to go home – now.'

'Eh? What's that? Melfort, isn't it? What's this all about? Fine thing if a man can't take a walk without –'

'What it is about doesn't concern you. Will you leave us, or must I persuade you further?'

Sheffield didn't like what he heard in the earl's voice and beat a hasty retreat, whilst Dunstone searched feverishly in his mind for something he had done which involved Melfort. As nothing occurred to him he went on the attack.

'What the devil do you think you're doing, sir? You've no right to accost me like this.'

'I have every right.' The earl's voice was soft and full of menace. 'You and I have something to settle.'

'I can't think what.' Rupert was growing uneasier by the second. Melfort wasn't a man to trifle with and his tone had sent a shiver up Dunstone's spine. 'How dare you molest me in such a way? We have nothing to talk about.'

'I haven't started to molest you yet, and we have much to talk about. Tell me how you forced Crystal Yorke to fit in with your plans. I would like to hear your version of that particular piece of malice.'

'Crystal Yorke?' The viscount heard the quaver in his own voice. 'Who is she and what has she got to do with you?'

'I love her and, because of what you did, I've lost her.'

Rupert gaped. He had had no idea that Corry's assistant had any connection with a man as highly-born and as dangerous as Melfort. But in spite of his shock and the dire position he was in, he continued to bluster, swearing he knew nothing about any plans, even pretending he hadn't heard of Crystal Yorke. He backed further and further away, still protesting, until a sinewy arm shot out and grabbed him by the collar.

'Brummell was right; you are a viper. And the best way to deal with a viper is to put one's heel on its neck.'

Stuart's first blow knocked Rupert flat on his back, but he didn't stay at rest for very long. Jerked to his feet,

Dunstone cried aloud as blow followed blow. His nose was bleeding, his mouth badly cut, his eye hinting at the bruise which was to come. But the earl hadn't yet finished.

Finally, Dunstone lay moaning on the cobblestones, begging for an end to the violence.

'Yes,' said Stuart, straightening his evening coat and adjusting the frill of his shirt sleeves. 'I think that will do. There is no way you can conceal your bruises, Somerset. Your father isn't blind, nor is he a fool. Go home and tell him why I did this. And by the way, I have a message for you from Brummell.'

But Rupert hardly heard it. His head was ringing, his whole body one gigantic, throbbing pain. He didn't know how he managed to get to his front door, but somehow he did. But there, even greater trouble awaited him.

Selkirk had caught Charlotte crying earlier that day and had had enough of mysteries, sternly demanding the truth from her. She had held out as long as she could, but for once Marcus shewed her no lenience. The whole truth spilled out through her sobs and when the viscount almost fell into the hall, his father was standing by the stairs looking as Rupert had never seen him look before.

After a very unpleasant half-hour Marcus said icily:

'You will go to Bath tonight. Our house there is not closed and the servants are still in residence. Your mother is to know nothing of this. I shall find some reason why you have decided to leave town in such a hurry without saying good-bye to her, but it won't be the truth. That might kill her, as I would like to kill you.'

'Father —'

'Don't call me that. You're no son of mine. You've been spoilt and pampered all your life and perhaps part of that is my fault. You thought me soft and easy-going. So I am usually, but there are things in life which are simply not done. Unwritten rules exist and you have broken them all many times. So far I've ignored your lapses, but what you did to that girl and old Corry is more than any decent man could stomach. Get out of my sight, and don't come back until I send for you.'

Rupert staggered to his room where two flunkeys with expressionless faces were packing his things. He flung himself into a chair, demanding brandy. Neither servant moved, but Rupert knew better than to strike them for their insolence. They were his father's emissaries and he had no power over them any longer.

He washed his face and changed his clothes, his violent rage beginning to grow stronger than his fright. The earl had terrified him; so had his father, for different reasons. Now there was just a desire for revenge and he spat at his reflection in the mirror as he dabbed at a cut which still oozed blood.

'I'll pay you ten times over for this, Melfort,' he said under his breath. 'I may have to wait, but my chance will come and then you'll be sorry you ever laid a hand on me.

'Blast you, Melfort, blast you! Before very long I'll see you in perdition.'

'I'm extremely sorry, my lord, but I don't know where Miss Yorke has gone.'

Basil had been shaken when the earl had approached him, even more surprised when he saw the deep unhappiness in Stuart. Corry had assumed that Crystal's lover was a ne'er-do-well, who had thrown her over on finding her pregnant, but clearly that wasn't the case. Basil found himself rapidly changing his judgment.

'You must have some idea. Corry, this is of vital importance to me.'

The earl's tribulation almost tempted Basil to tell the

truth; then he remembered his promise to Crystal and shook his head.

'No, sir, I have none.'

'Dear God! If only you knew – no, I'm sorry. I have no right to impose my troubles on you. But I would ask this. If you hear from Miss Yorke, please let me know.'

'I doubt if she will write to me.'

'But if she does.'

'Very well, my lord. I will do what I can.'

Corry watched the earl go, recalling the first occasion on which Crystal had seen Melfort. He, Basil, had warned her against dallying with the aristocracy, but she hadn't listened. Yet her *affaire* with Stuart Haversham had been no light thing. She had loved him; Basil had seen the supreme joy in her. Now he had seen the agony in the earl and knew that Stuart had loved just as passionately.

It was easy now to see what had happened. Corry had heard that the earl had gone to Scotland for a month. He must have returned earlier than expected and found Crystal in the role into which Somerset had forced her, drawing false conclusions.

Whilst Corry sighed over the pity of it all, the earl reached home to find an urgent message from his father. His mother had become ill again, her condition so serious that Stuart had no choice but to go to her. She was asking for him and it was a duty he couldn't shirk.

As he was unable to search for Crystal himself, he left the matter in the hands of his capable and confidential valet.

'Get as many men as you need,' he said to James Porter as he donned his coat. 'You'll find money in the desk – ample to pay your agents. Keep in touch with me, won't you?'

'Of course, my lord.'

Porter was a stalwart young man with a keen eye and

sharp wits. He had known at once when his master had abandoned high-born prostitutes for a woman he really loved. He had wondered who she was and now he knew. James wasn't in the least critical. Love could strike at any man, even the light-hearted earl, only now Melfort was no longer light of heart. His face was haggered, his eyes betrayed his grief.

'I'm grateful to you, James.'

'Leave it all to me, m'lord. I know a few men used to this kind of work. We'll find her for you.'

And with that the earl had to be satisfied, getting into the waiting coach and ordering the driver to set off. He leaned back against the leather seat, closing his eyes and seeing Crystal's face as clearly as if she were sitting opposite him.

'Where are you, my love?' he whispered, the lines at the corners of his mouth etched even more deeply. 'Crystal, my dearest dear. Where in the name of God have you gone?'

It didn't take Crystal and Fanny long to put the late Thomas Brett's shop and living accommodation to rights.

Plenty of hot water, soap, elbow-grease and will-power transformed the place within two weeks. A new board hung outside the shop. It had gold lettering on shiny black paint, with C. Yorke inscribed boldly for all to see.

With sparkling windows inviting people to draw near, it was only a matter of time before they stepped over the threshold, exclaiming at the gleaming counters and shelves, the new labels on the well-scrubbed jars and, most of all, at the delightful array of enamelled snuff boxes set out on dark red velvet.

Crystal had found the book Mrs Shuttle had spoken of and, when she wasn't busy serving or painting, she pored over the faded pages, eager for knowledge. She read how snuff was prepared, the most expensive sort being made of the soft parts of the best kind of manufactured leaf tobacco. Well dried previous to grinding, frequently sifted so that the precious dust should not become too fine, it was moistened several times throughout the process with rose or orange water.

She learned the names of other snuffs, many to be found on her own shelves. Havre, French Carotte, Domingo, Arras, Violet Strasbourg being just a few. She read pages devoted to the scents used to mix with snuff: musk, essences of oils of bermagot, cloves, lavender, otto of roses, orange flowers, jasmins and rose leaves. There were instructions, too, in Thomas's crabbed writing, not to be over-lavish with the amount of perfume used, nor let the snuff become dry. Warning was given also not to take it unless the chill was off it.

The business began to flourish and that meant harder work for Crystal because her painted boxes became very popular. Fanny would exhort her to remember the baby as she wielded a paint brush long after midnight. Crystal didn't heed her. She wanted to drown herself in work so that she didn't have to think of Stuart and their brutal parting. But labouring into the early hours of the morning didn't take the pain away, nor did it dim the remembrance of his face. She loved him as much as ever, hiding her affliction as she put on a bright face to greet her customers when daytime came.

She displayed only one of Corry's boxes at a time, a piece of wisdom she had learnt from him. Many admired the delicate object, but no one bought it for the price was too rich for their blood.

After a while, Crystal realised that she would have to go out and seek the aristocracy when more money was needed. Fanny had been right. It had been expensive to renovate the shop and make the rooms above comfortable and Corry's generous gift was wilting fast. Even though she was doing well, funds would soon have to be found for fresh, and far from cheap, supplies. The roof had sprung a leak, and there was always food to be paid for.

In spite of all that had happened, Crystal was as lovely as ever, impending motherhood giving her a special glow. Many a man's eyes lit up when she weighed their snuff on the brass scales and she had learned not to be embarrassed by the compliments she received.

Everyone around had accepted her story that she was a widow of a soldier and all treated her with respect.

Then one day a customer who knew rather more of her history strolled into the shop. Crystal was putting back one of the jars on the shelf, not noticing him enter.

'Rather heavy for you I would have thought, Miss Yorke.'

Crystal turned, her colour draining away as she stared at George Brummell.

He raised his hat politely and favoured her with a smile, warmer than any of his acquaintances ever received.

'Sir!'

'I do hope you are not going to swoon,' he said in mild alarm. 'I've never learnt what to do with swooning women.'

Crystal got hold of herself, anger flooding through her as she remembered Brummell's part in her predicament.

'You are not welcome here, sir,' she said sharply. 'I would like you to go at once.'

The Beau perched himself on a stool near the counter and gave a rare laugh.

'I daresay you would, but I'm not running off yet. I have something to tell you.'

'I don't want to hear it.'

'That's unfortunate because you're going to listen whether you like it or not.' The amusement in Brummell died and Crystal could see his eyes harden. 'I now know the truth about what happened and understand your marked distaste for me when we first met. I had no part in what happened, I assure you. All Dunstone asked me that day in Corry's shop was what sort of box to buy his mother. I have many faults, although I've never admitted them before and never will again, but blackmailing helpless women isn't one of them.'

Crystal held on to the counter, her heart thudding.

'The viscount lied?'

'Dunstone invariably lies.'

'Does –?'

'– Stuart know? Yes, he does. When he found out what really took place he half killed Dunstone. His mother is very ill again so he's had to return to Scotland but, as I understand it, he's got agents searching the length and breadth of the land for you.'

'He mustn't find me! You won't tell him, will you?' Then Crystal paused. 'How did you know I was here? Mr Corry didn't tell you, did he?'

'No, at least, not exactly. I pressed the cunning old fox so hard that in the end he suggested I should go and see the delights of the Avon Gorge, a thing I have no intention of doing. I should find the whole thing far too fatiguing and geographical wonders have never interested me.'

'He promised he wouldn't tell anyone.'

'Nor did he, precisely, as I've said. But I had to see you, Miss Yorke.' The Beau was serious again. 'I couldn't let you go on thinking that I'd done such a thing to you and I had to let you know what Melfort feels for you.'

Crystal drew back.

'I know what his lordship feels for me,' she said sourly. 'He made it very plain.'

'He didn't understand.'

'He didn't want to understand.'

'Then you won't see him?'

'No. Sir, I beg you not to speak of this shop or where I am.'

Brummell considered Crystal for a moment or two. She was utterly ravishing, but Melfort couldn't marry her and perhaps she was wise not to re-open old wounds.

'Very well. My word is given. And now, since I'm here, I would like to make a purchase.'

'Of course, sir.' Crystal was the shopkeeper again, personal problems thrust away until she was alone once more. 'Some snuff perhaps? I have a very good one here, delivered only this morning.'

'Not snuff. I'll have Corry's silver box. Oh yes, I recognise it. I often considered buying it when I visited Swan Street, but somehow never did.'

'You don't have to.' Crystal was diffident. 'It's rather expensive.'

'So was the mistake I made.'

'But you didn't make the mistake. It was the earl who did that and I won't take your money.'

'Then I shall steal the box, madam.'

They stared at each other, neither budging. Then Crystal gave a small laugh.

'I'd heard you like to get your own way, Mr Brummell.'

'Yes I do. Here is my money. Now give me my goods, Miss Yorke.'

She put Benjamin's masterpiece into the Beau's hand with a shy smile.

'I hope it pleases.'

'It does. My dear, are you sure you don't want to see Melfort?'

'I have never been surer of anything in my life. It's over, Mr Brummell; quite finished.'

He gave a slight sigh.

'Then I shall return to London, for the Bristol air is not to my liking. Thank you for this. I shall treasure it. I've only seen one thing more exquisitely designed in my pursuit of perfection.'

'And what was that.'

'Why you, of course, Miss Yorke. What else?'

With that the Beau moved unhurriedly to the door closing it gently behind him. He glanced up and down Christmas Steps, deciding against further exploration and getting into his carriage.

'Really Stuart,' he said aloud, uncaring whether the coachman heard or not. 'What a fool you are. If she'd been mine I'd never have let her get away.'

'Pardon, sir?'

'I wasn't talking to you, my good man,' said Brummell tartly. 'Be so good as to pay attention to the road. I wish to return to London with all speed, but in one piece. I've had enough of this benighted place to last me a lifetime.

'And oblige me by not chattering any more. I am going to take a nap.'

Nine

The Earl of Melfort had been at Fort Ullen for two months before the marquis decided to find our why his son looked liked a man on the brink of hell.

'It's not just because of your mother, is it?' he asked as he and Stuart walked along the banks of Loch Shinn. 'There's something else wrong. Can you tell me about it?'

Stuart was feeling very low that morning. Porter had had no news for him and time was passing quickly. The thought of Crystal blotted out everything else for him, the fact that she was to have his child turning the screw inside him to the point of explosion.

He hadn't intended to tell the marquis what had happened, but human weakness made the need to share his tribulation too strong to overcome.

'I think I must,' he said finally, 'or I shall go out of my mind.'

Ravenmore gave Stuart a sharp look. The anguish in the earl and the hurt in his eyes were very real and not brought about by some trivial problem.

'Well, I have a close mouth, as you know. What is it, Stuart?'

When the earl had told his father every last detail, the marquis's mouth was a hard, straight line.

'Thank God I haven't got a son like Rupert Somerset.

And you really love this girl, Crystal?'

'With all my heart, sir. I would die for her.'

'That wouldn't help much, would it? I suppose I ought to try to stop you, but stopping a Haversham is no light task. I agree that you and Charlotte should go your separate ways, but a painter of snuff-boxes!'

Melfort stopped, his voice terse.

'Be careful what you say, father. I don't care what she does. She's all I'll ever need and you were right. True love does exist. I know that now, but it's too late.'

'I'm always careful what I say,' returned the marquis smoothly. 'And when you do find my future daughter-in-law, tell her I'd like a gold snuff-box with an English garden painted on the lid round the initials G.A.'

'G.A?' Stuart was diverted momentarily. 'But mother's name is – oh – I see.'

'I'm glad you do.'

Suddenly the meaning of his father's earlier words brought a gleam of hope to Stuart and he said quickly:

'Does that mean you will give your consent to our marriage?'

'I suppose I'll have to. It's a monumental mésalliance, but can I stop you?'

'No, my lord. I'd go to the far ends of the earth if she would come with me.'

'Then my choices are limited. Running our estates from China, or some such far-flung place, is scarcely practical. Yes, you have my consent. I turned love away once. I won't force you to do the same, but in the circumstances I suggest that the pair of you go abroad for a while. Give people time to forget Lady Jane Markham.'

'I don't know what to say.'

'Say nothing until you hear the favour I am about to seek from you. No, beg would be a better word.'

'Favour? Anything, father.'

'You won't like it, I warn you. It will tie you here when you long to be off searching for your girl. Stuart, I have never loved your mother, as you are aware, and I have always felt some remorse because of it. I owe her something for all the years we have been together, during which I have given her but a small part of myself. But you, m'dear, are the only one who can pay that debt for me.'

'I'm not sure that I understand.'

'I want you to stay here until your mother dies, and she is going to die, you know. She has a cancer which is eating her up, but even the good Dr Laurie can't say how long it will be before the end. It could be months – perhaps a year. She's fighting hard, you see. I think she knew from the start that her illness was terminal. That's when she asked me to send for you. She is always talking of you, asking whether you are in the house or out walking. She will need you even more as time goes by.'

Melfort's heart sank. His father was right. It could be many months before he was free to leave Scotland, but he loved his mother and had seen her eyes light up whenever he had gone to her bedside. The marquis had never asked him for anything before and had just given him a gift of such magnitude that it had almost taken his breath away.

He hadn't expected his father to countenance a marriage between Crystal and himself. Now, Ravenmore had broken all rules and traditions and accepted a girl of humble origin whom he'd never seen.

Stuart met his father's questioning glance and nodded.

'Very well, my lord. I will stay.'

'Thank you. I know what it must have cost you to agree. You have people looking for Miss Yorke?'

'Yes, but Porter has sent no word so far.'

'I know a man in London; very astute and experienced.

I'll write to him. Later, you can give me such facts as I am free to use. Don't give up hope. We'll find her.'

'I pray it will be soon. The baby –'

'My grandchild. How old that makes me feel, but I expect I shall get used to it. Human beings are very adaptable.'

'And if we can't find her – ever – ?'

'I refuse to consider such a possibility. Damn it, boy, we are Havershams. Nothing is impossible for us. Now let's turn back. Your mother will be asking for you and don't let her see your pain. She's got enough of her own to contend with. Poor Hildegarde. Who would have thought that that pretty girl I met so long ago would have a terrible end like this?'

Crystal was growing near to her time. In spite of Fanny's continued scoldings she was still working hard, painting her boxes, selling snuff, and visiting the rich in the outlying suburbs of Bristol to shew them Basil's boxes. She had sold two of them by this method and soon another would have to go. She wasn't sure what she was going to do when the last had gone, but her takings were increasing each week and she refused to be pessimistic about the future.

She had become friendly with her fellow shopkeepers over the months. There was Miss Sibyl Daley, selling tea and coffee; Mr Johnson, who kept a bookshop and writing materials, and Mr Jaffe, with his selection of fine china and glass.

There was also David Dunhill, a hatter, who had given Crystal a good deal of help in the early days. He was a broad-shouldered man of some thirty years, personable in appearance and well spoken. But lately he had grown rather too attentive for Crystal's liking.

She had welcomed his friendship at first, but when she

saw the way he was looking at her she began to avoid him, becoming rather cool if he entered her shop. She wanted nothing to do with a man seeking love, for she had none left to return. Stuart had taken every last drop of hers and had thrown it back in her face.

Her world was still filled with Melfort. He never left her thoughts or her dreams and she knew he never would. When his child was born it would be even more difficult to drive his image away and she sighed as she picked up another box and began to paint.

But David Dunhill had no intention of being put off by Crystal's recent rebuffs. His business was losing money fast, his creditors pressing him hard for money. The snuff shop was doing well and Dunhill had calculated almost to a penny what the weekly takings were. To acquire such a thriving and growing concern, along with a comely wife, was the complete answer to his predicament.

He wasn't worried about the child soon to be born. Children could be ignored or, if the new arrival proved to be a nuisance, an accident wouldn't be hard to arrange.

Crystal's son didn't hurry into the world. Her labour was long and filled with the kind of pain she hadn't known existed. Fanny and the midwife hovered round her, bathing her forehead, encouraging her, praying for a safe delivery.

When the boy was born the midwife shook her head, but not where Crystal could see her concern. The baby was small and weak, its cry feeble. But to Crystal he was perfect and in spite of her exhaustion she was bathed in happiness as she held the tiny infant against her breast. He was part of Stuart and thus doubly precious to her. In her joy, she didn't notice that the baby, whom she called Hamish, wasn't a lusty one. He was in her arms and that was all which mattered.

Two months later, Dunhill asked Crystal to marry him.

'I'm afraid that is out of the question, sir,' she said shortly. 'I am sensible of the honour you pay me, but I have no wish to wed again.'

'I pray that you will reconsider.' Dunhill was perspiring, trying to hide his eagerness and impatience. More bills had flooded in that morning and ruin was staring him in the face. 'You need someone to look after you and the child.'

'I am quite capable of looking after myself and my son.'

'But you would find it easier with a man behind you to protect you.'

'I have managed extremely well so far.' Crystal didn't like the way Dunhill was moving towards her. 'I shall continue to do so and now I'd like you to go, if you please.'

When he grabbed her, Crystal struck him hard across the face.

'Get out, you money-grubbing monster. I once thought you a friend, but now I see what you are really like. You want this shop, don't you? I've heard the rumours about your financial problems, but you're not going to use me to solve them.'

'You damned bitch!' Dunhill stopped pretending, his hand tight about Crystal's wrist. 'So high and mighty, aren't you? You were glad enough to have me running errands for you when you hadn't a customer to your name. Seems to me you owe me something.'

'I owe you nothing and let go of me or I shall scream.'

'Scream away.' His voice thickened. 'It's not just your money I want. You're a beautiful woman, you know. Now give me a kiss and say you'll think again.'

Crystal's free hand reached along the counter until she found one of the heavy weights used for large quantities of snuff. Dunhill yelled as she hit him over the head with it, falling to his knees as blood began to drip down his forehead and into his eyes.

'Now will you go?' demanded Crystal, concealing her alarm. 'Or must I give you another taste of this? You are contemptible and I'll make it my business to let everyone know what kind of man you are.'

After Dunhill had groped his way out of the shop, swearing revenge, Crystal leaned against the counter shaking in every limb. She had had a near-escape and she knew it. Fanny was out doing the marketing, and it was a quiet time as far as customers were concerned. Gradually she steadied herself, wiping the iron weight and going to the small store behind the shop where there was a jug of water and a bowl.

A small mirror hung over the side table and she looked at the reflection of her ashen face and dilated pupils. It had been a bad experience, but she had to get over it quickly. She had a shop to run and a child to rear.

By now she had realised just how delicate Hamish was. He seldom cried, as if he hadn't the strength to do so, and often when she watched him sleep it seemed to her that his skin was almost transparent.

She didn't think the hatter would bother her again. The ugly incident was over, but some of Dunhill's words still hammered into her brain. She did need a man, but only one would do for her and she was sick at heart as she dried her hands.

'It's you I need, Stuart,' she whispered, 'but I'm never going to see you again. Oh, my love, will I ever stop wanting you so much?'

That evening Crystal's shop was burnt to the ground. She was out, visiting Lord and Lady Templeton, who had expressed a desire to see one of her silver boxes. As she grew near to Christmas Steps she saw the flames, feeling icy cold inside when she saw that it was her property which was crackling away merrily like a bonfire.

She screamed in frenzy as she saw Fanny leaning out of one of the upstairs windows, a bundle in her arms.

'Hamish! Oh God, Hamish! Someone help me. That's my baby. Fanny, jump! Jump, for pity's sake. There are people here to catch you.'

Those who had gathered round cried out in agreement, but Fanny seemed deaf to them. Carefully, she threw Hamish down to the neighbours, satisfied when she saw the infant caught in the strong arms of the local butcher.

'Now you, Fanny, now you!' Crystal had taken Hamish, holding him tightly to her. 'Dear Fanny, jump! Jump!'

But Fanny Bethall had left it too late. The spectators gasped in horror as the girl's hair caught alight and tongues of orange seared her face and arms. She tried to climb on to the window cill but the furnace beat her back into the room and her shrieks were the most terrible sounds Crystal had ever heard.

The next morning Crystal gazed at the ashes of her hopes. All that she possessed had been in the shop, save for the boxes she had had on her when she went to the Templetons'. She had lost most of her wordly goods, but much worse. She had lost a dear and loving friend.

She would have to write to Basil and tell him about Fanny. She had kept in touch with him, telling him of Hamish's arrival, but not how poorly the baby was. She wouldn't tell him about the fire either. He had given her enough and this time she had to stand on her own feet.

'Come away, my pet,' said Miss Daley, who had taken Crystal and Hamish into her home the night before. 'There's nothing you can do now. They've caught that dreadful man Dunhill. He was seen outside your shop before the fire started and he's admitted his crime. He claims that he didn't know what he was doing because he was so drunk, but no one's likely to swallow that tale. I've watched him eyeing you up and down. I suppose you sent him packing.'

'Something like that,' replied Crystal drearily. 'It's all gone. I was so proud of it, but now it's just a pile of smouldering wood. And my poor Fanny. She was so dear to me. What am I going to do now?'

But later that day a solution came to Crystal as she sat in Miss Daley's second bedroom nursing Hamish. The boxes still left would have to be sold quickly and below their true value if necessary.

She had heard of a place of dubious reputation on the outskirts of the town where people gambled for high stakes.

'Women as well as men,' Sibyl had once said in a shocked voice. 'What sort of women would go to such a sink of iniquity?'

Crystal knew the answer to that now. She would go, with such money as she could raise. She would gamble and pray that Fortune would smile on her and her cards as it had done once before. She had won handsomely when she had played at Lady Mercier's. She had to try to do the same again.

Her future and that of her delicate son hung on her success. It was a frightening thought. One's whole life, and that of another, dependent on the turn of a card, but it couldn't be helped. She straightened her shoulders and looked down at the sleeping child.

'Don't worry, my blessing,' she said softly. 'I'll do it for us. I'm a survivor. I just pray to God that you are, too.'

Two days before Crystal set out to try her luck, Peter Heslop called on her at Miss Daley's.

'We've not met before,' he said, shuffling his feet uncomfortably, 'but Fanny Bethall was my girl.'

'I know. She often spoke of you.' Crystal was stony. 'It's a pity you didn't remember that when she was in trouble.'

'Yes.' He made no excuses, just raising his shoulders helplessly. 'I was so angry when Fan told me what 'ad 'appened I reckon I lost me 'ead. Took a fair time for me to see that she'd never do nowt like that from choice.'

'Well, you've left it a bit too late, haven't you?'

'Seems so. She wrote to me once. Told me never to mention to a soul where she were stayin'. I didn't anwer 'cos I can't write. 'Ad to git someone to read the note to me as it was. Then, quite sudden like, I knew I 'ad to see 'er and tell 'er I were sorry, but when I got to the shop it weren't there no more. A man told me Fan 'ad died in the fire.'

'She did and she would never have been in the place at all if you hadn't turned your back on her. She'd have stayed in London and been safe. She worshipped you, you – Mr Heslop!'

The tears were running down Peter's face and Crystal's condemnation was finished.

'My dear, don't, don't. I didn't mean to go on at you like that, but I loved Fanny, too, and I miss her intolerably. I was just hitting out at you.'

'Right that you should.' Heslop wiped his nose with his sleeve. 'It were my fault, like you said.'

'No, it wasn't. If anyone is to blame it was the man who raped Fanny. But for him, none of this would have happened.'

'I want 'is name.'

Heslop's tone had changed abruptly. The tears were gone and his eyes were a hard, bright blue.

'No.' Crystal was very definite. 'I'm not going to tell you. If I did, you'd only get yourself into trouble.'

'Mebbe, mebbe not. Just tell us 'oo it were.'

'I've told you I won't. If you can get someone else to tell you, so be it, but I won't be a party to what you intend to do. I cared for Fanny far too much for that.'

He nodded.

'All right. I knows you mean well, but it won't stop me. I'll find another way and in the end I'll get him.'

'And when you do find him I suppose you'll knock him half senseless.'

Heslop turned at the door.

'No, Miss Yorke, there'll be no 'alf-way about it. When I find out 'oo did that to my Fan I'm going to bloody well kill the bastard.'

Crystal hated the dark, smelly house into which she was grudgingly admitted upon shewing that she had sufficient money to play at the tables.

It stank of stale beer, the floor was dirty, the tables hadn't seen a cloth for months. Potmen were serving drinks to those crouched over their cards, slopping ale and wine in their carelessness. No one seemed to be bothered. All the players could see was the money in front of them and the hands they held.

Crystal was led to a table, hardly noticing who sat there. She hadn't expected the place to be like a club in St James's, but neither had she thought to find such a seedy hole with an aura of evil hanging over everything.

When she sat down she felt every ounce of strength drain from her as she saw the face of the man sitting opposite her.

Rupert Somerset had found Bath exceedingly tedious. The family house was as quiet as a grave and the town full of old men with gout taking the waters. He had soon got to hear of Reeve's, the gambling den in Bristol, and became a regular patron. In a way he would be quite sorry to leave it, but as at last he had been summoned home by his father, that would probably be his last night there.

The sight of Crystal Yorke filled him first with utter astonishment and then a warm glow of contentment which he found hard to conceal.

He hadn't forgotten a single blow which Melfort had given him, nor the fact that the girl staring at him in horror had been the earl's mistress.

He could hardly believe that the gods had put such a prize into his lap, for now he could strike both at the Yorke woman and the man who had made him grovel and plead for mercy.

At first he merely inclined his head, his mind busy with plans. It was no use denouncing the girl as a whore; most of the women present were whores. Then the answer came to him, easily and simply, and he smiled as he nodded to the dealer for another card.

Crystal tried to keep her mind on the play, for it was vital that she won. She had only been able to find a buyer for one of the boxes and then she'd got a smaller price than she'd hoped for.

To add to her already dire straits, another disaster had befallen her on her way home from the house of the purchaser. Ruffians had fallen on her as she crossed a lonely stretch of the Downs. They had seized her reticule, containing the last of Benjamin's boxes, throwing her to the ground with triumphant laughs.

She had wept that night, feeling terribly alone and nearer to hopelessness than she'd ever been before. Her shop was gone, Fanny was dead, her last source of income snatched from her. Only the money from her customer, which she had concealed in her bodice, remained.

It wasn't until Hamish began to whimper that she stopped feeling sorry for herself and had picked him up, opening the front of her gown to feed him.

'I'm sorry, sweetest,' she had said, fresh tears in her eyes when she had seen how hard it was for her son to suck. 'I promise I won't give up. I'll get us out of this somehow.'

But now, with Viscount Dunstone's eyes watching her every move, she wasn't so sure that she was going to be able to keep her word. Brummell had told her that Stuart had given Somerset a thrashing. Now the viscount had found her again and it wasn't difficult to read his intentions. He couldn't touch the earl, but he had her pinned down in his venomous grasp. Given a hand like that, Rupert Somerset would play it up to the skies.

At first her luck held. It seemed too good to be true as she watched the pile of sovereigns in front of her grow larger. Then she saw Somerset's smile and her stomach tightened into knots. He was losing to her, yet he was smiling. The feeling of dread increased and she knew it was only a matter of time before Rupert made his move.

When it came it made her jump, for the viscount's voice was suddenly raised in anger as he called the owner to come to his table.

'Here, Reeve, what's wrong with you?'

Herbert Reeve, a thin, ageing man with bent shoulders and an enduring love of money, hurried over to the viscount, bowing low.

'My lord, what is it? Is the ale flat?'

'I've no idea. I don't drink the filthy stuff. No, why do you allow known cheats in here? This woman's face has been teasing my memory for some time, but now I've placed her. She's a sharp one and has been thrown out of most of the gambling dens in London. Look at what she's accumulated and all of it taken from innocent men who didn't see what she was doing.'

The others round the table began to rumble with displeasure and worse, Rupert fanning their wrath.

'Are you going to let her stay and milk us of every last penny?'

'My lord, my lord, I'd no idea. I would never have

allowed such a creature to be admitted if I'd known her history. She had money and so I let her in.'

'Well, you'd better get rid of her now, hadn't you? And don't let her take her ill-gotten gains with her. Those we'll share between us, don't you agree, gentlemen?'

The roar of approval was unanimous and at a motion of Reeve's hand, Crystal found herself dragged off her feet by the huge bully kept by the proprietor for the sole purpose of disposing of trouble-makers.

She struggled hard, but the man was a mountain of flesh, and the next moment she hit the cobbles with a sickening thud which knocked the breath out of her.

As Rupert Somerset sank back in his chair, eyes half closed in satisfaction, Crystal managed to get to her feet and return to Miss Daley's.

It was the last night she would be able to shelter there. With regret and sadness, Sibyl had told her that her sister was coming to live with her and the spare room would be needed.

Crystal got upstairs without Sibyl hearing her, washing her hands and face and brushing her torn gown. Then she looked down at Hamish and her heart contracted. His fever was obvious, the weak motions of his hands telling the whole story.

'Dearest,' she murmured, touching the small, hot cheek. 'I couldn't do it after all. I'm sorry, my lamb, so very sorry. But I haven't given up yet and I never will. They're looking for someone to help in the kitchens at The Bull and Bear. I'll go and see the landlord tomorrow. At least it would be a roof over our heads, if they'll have me, and I'll never let them take you to the workhouse.'

But the next day the landlord eyed Crystal dubiously.

'Didn't reckon on an infant,' he said discouragingly. 'You don't look all that strong neither. The job's 'ard.'

'I'm stronger than I look and I don't mind how many hours I work. Hamish won't be a nuisance; he never cries.'

The landlord, one Joseph Wheelwright, scratched his head.

'Well, I don't know –' He was torn between common sense and the pleading look in Crystal's eyes. She was thin and grubby, but she was a beauty, too, and that might please his customers.

But it wasn't until Mrs Betsy Wheelwright bustled out that the matter was settled. She listened to her husband, took one look at Hamish, and said firmly:

'Of course you can have the job, lass. Come on inside and I'll get you a bite to eat. You look as if you could use something. The bairn's ill, isn't he?'

'Very ill, I'm afraid, but I've no money for a doctor.'

'Dr Fenner likes to call in here of an evening for a tot of rum. We'll get him to look at the poor mite. What's his name?'

'Hamish. Mine is Crystal Yorke.'

'And the father?'

Crystal was going to tell the story she had first used upon reaching Bristol, but when she looked into Mrs Wheelwright's concerned face she knew she couldn't lie again.

'He hasn't got one.'

'Thought not. Dratted men. Pity some of 'em were ever born. Well, go on, Joe, get back to the bar. Half your stock'll be gone if you don't keep an eye on them potmen. And you, m'dear, there's a small attic room you can use. Not a palace, but always kept spotlessly clean, if I do say so myself.'

'I don't know how to thank you.' Crystal was weakened by kindness as she had been once before. 'I wasn't sure you'd let me keep Hamish here.'

'Lord above! Separate a sick baby from its mother? Never heard of such a thing. Here, drink this hot tea and take a slice of pie. I've got a good hand with a pie, although I says it who shouldn't.'

'It's a beautiful pie,' said Crystal, hardly able to swallow a mouthful. 'And you're beautiful, too, Mrs Wheelwright.'

'What? Me beautiful? No one's ever said that of me in all me born days. Beautiful, indeed!'

'You are inside and that's where it counts.'

Mrs Wheelwright stopped smiling.

'Aye, you're right. Your looks haven't done you much good, have they, but my guess is that you're sound all through. Here's a long life to you and your Hamish.'

Their cups touched in the toast. Then Crystal said sadly:

'Thank you, but I don't think Hamish is going to get better.'

Betsy wiped her eyes furtively with the bottom of her apron.

'Then let's wish him well while he's here, shall we?'

'Yes.' Crystal looked down at the child she had wanted so much and nodded. 'Yes, we can do that. To you, Hamish Yorke. Be happy, my little love, be happy – until it's time for you to go.'

Ten

Rupert Somerset's first mistake upon reaching London was to get drunk. His second was to return late in the evening to regale his sister with the triumph he had enjoyed at Reeve's gambling den.

Charlotte was rigid with fury, her voice a contemptuous lash.

'You are despicable, Rupert. You lied to me and I'll never forgive you for that. Give me the money which Crystal won – all of it.'

'Damned if I will.' Dunstone lurched to a chair, clutching at the back of it for support. 'What's the matter with you, Charlie? Lost your sense of humour?'

'No, but I've found my sense of justice, if somewhat belatedly. Give it to me, or I'll go to father and tell him what you've done.'

'No, you won't. He wouldn't believe you anyway.'

'You don't think so?' Charlotte was more biting still. 'I think he will, and consider this. The estate may be entailed, but father isn't old and he has the constitution of an ox. You could be a penniless outcast for many years to come. The money, please.'

Once she had dealt with her brother, Charlotte sent a message to the earl, now back in town.

They met in the duchess's room, for Her Grace had

declined to go home until after Charlotte's wedding. It wasn't only the forthcoming celebration which made Annabel stay. She was finding the dramas going on about her rather bracing. She had rejoiced when Rupert had been banished and had had an exhilarating passage-of-arms with Louis-Rey, which she had won hands down.

Upon hearing that Charlotte was to inherit the duchess's fortune, Louis-Rey had promptly withdrawn his offer of marriage. After comforting Charlotte, who was in floods of tears, Annabel had sent for John and demanded an explanation of his extraordinary behaviour.

'You must see, Your Grace,' he had said quietly but firmly, 'that I cannot wed Charlotte now that she is one day to become one of the richest women in London.'

'In England and what's that got to do with anything?'

'I'm not a fortune-hunter.'

'No one said you were.'

'It will be said if I marry your heiress.'

'Don't talk such utter balderdash, man. She hasn't suddenly turned from the woman you love into an heiress. She's Charlie. What's the matter with you?'

But Annabel's strictures hadn't moved Louis-Rey so she had had to fall back on guile.

'Very well; that's simple. I shall change my Will.'

'I cannot let Charlotte make such a sacrifice for me.'

'She won't be making a sacrifice. You haven't heard what the terms of my new Will are to be.'

Louis-Rey had been in despair at the thought of losing Charlotte, but he saw no way out of the dilemma. She was, as she had always been, too good for him in every way.

'Whatever the terms, Your Grace, I cannot see that they will help.'

'Oh can't you? Well, not many men have much imagination so I suppose I can't hold that against you. I shall leave half of my worldly goods to Charlotte and the other half to you. And, Mr John Louis-Rey, you can stop looking at me like that because there isn't a damn thing you can do to stop me. Now go and tell Charlotte to call in the dressmakers. I'm sick to death of her snivels.'

And now the handsome Earl of Melfort was kissing her hand as if she were a twenty-year-old. She gave him a coquettish look, waiting impatiently to hear the details of Rupert's latest infamy.

'I'll call him out.' Melfort's face was like granite. 'This time a beating won't do. I'll put a bullet through him.'

'No.' Charlotte held up her hand to stem Stuart's rage. 'He's a poor shot and you're one of the best in the country. Everyone knows that and it would damage your reputation if you killed him. He's not worth your good name.'

'Quite right, Melfort.' Annabel produced her fourth snuff box of the day, taking a generous pinch. 'Why waste your energy on a worm like Rupert? Go and find your girl.'

'She might be anywhere by now.'

'Stuart, use your head,' said Charlotte, exchanging an exasperated look with Annabel. 'She was in Bristol until recently, wasn't she? That much at least we learned from Rupert. Start from there.'

'But –'

It was the duchess's turn to click her tongue.

'Men are such blockheads. I wonder why they're so sure they're the superior sex. Charlie's right, my lord. Be off with you, or you really will lose her.'

'Do you think Crystal will forgive Stuart, even if he finds her?' Having sent the earl on his way, Charlotte was beginning to have doubts. 'She said she was quite done with him.'

Annabel tittered.

'He might have a rough time of it at first and serve him

right. But if she loves him, and I expect she does, he'll get her in the end.'

'Why do you assume that she still loves him?'

'She'd be a fool not to. He's a very attractive young rake. I rather fancy him myself.'

'Yes, Aunt Belle, I noticed you didn't pretend to be deaf for Stuart's benefit.'

'Enough of your impudence, Charlotte Somerset. You're getting above yourself, just because I've made your stubborn John see sense at last.'

Even the mention of John's name, and the certainty that he would soon be her husband, didn't erase Charlotte's frown.

'I do hope it works out. I'm so much to blame for all this.'

'Stop castigating yourself, you ninny, and fetch the cards. I don't feel in the least sleepy and you'd better not be either. There's nothing like a few games of faro to settle one down to the end of a busy day, don't you agree?'

'All the same if you don't. That's what we're going to play.'

As soon as Stuart reached Bristol he went to see a friend of his, Lord Stephen Harman, who had a charming villa at the foot of the Clifton Downs.

It didn't take Lord Stephen long to find out where Crystal had gone. He had many connections and within a few hours Melfort walked into The Bull and Bear. It was a friendly inn, warm and welcoming and clean. Mr Wheelwright wasn't used to customers of such quality as the earl, but he wasn't overawed by him either.

Stuart was drinking some rather good beer when he saw Crystal descending the stairs and making her way through a door at the rear.

Crystal turned quickly when she heard her name,

ravaged inside by conflicting emotions. She hadn't expected to see Stuart again and his mere presence weakened her. For his part, the earl was horrified by Crystal's appearance.

The eyes were as green as ever, but no longer sparkling. The red hair was as wondrously shining as he remembered it, but the face around which it fell was bleached. The rose had gone from the lips which had once met his so eagerly. The sweet curves of the body he had held against his own had vanished, too.

He was trying to think of the right thing to say when Crystal put an end to the silence.

'Go away, my lord,' she said tautly. 'You're too late. If you had wanted to see your son you should have come sooner. He died three days ago. He was never very strong and I couldn't give him the things he needed.'

Although her words were meant to wound, Crystal was overwhelmed by the desire to throw herself into Stuart's arms and cry her heart out for their lost baby. She could still see the tiny face, waxed and still. The sight of it ground into her soul and gave her sufficient anger to overcome her frailty. She would never give Stuart the opportunity of seeing her agony.

'He's dead?'

Melfort's voice was flat, and there was a numbness in his mind as he tried to accept what Crystal was saying.

'I've just told you he is. He was small and weak at birth and he couldn't take the nourishment I offered, not that that was much. Perhaps I killed him.'

'Don't!' The earl stretched out a hand, wanting Crystal so much that his longing made him catch his breath. 'Of course you didn't kill him. If it was anyone's fault that he didn't live it was mine. I learned the truth about what you were forced to do, but too late. Then I had to stay in Scotland for months because my mother was dying and needed me.'

Crystal ignored the hand which she yearned to cling to.

'I needed you, too,' she retorted bitterly, 'but you weren't there. I'm glad your mother was more fortunate. It must have been worth dying to keep you at her side for so long.'

Melfort closed his eyes, her words stabbing him like knives.

'You have every right to hate me. I was blind, foolish, hot-headed and unjust.'

'It doesn't matter any more.'

'It does to me. What did you call the child?'

'Hamish, but that's none of your concern, sir.'

'Yes it is; he was my son.'

'A pity you didn't remember that earlier.'

'I didn't know of your condition when we met that last time.'

'Would it have made any difference?' Crystal was as cold as ever. 'I doubt it. You would probably have asked which man fathered my bastard.'

'Dear God, don't do this to us.'

'Why not? And if you are offended by the truth I suggest you leave.'

'I shan't leave until you agree to come with me.'

'Then you will grow old and grey sitting in this pot-house, for I have no intention of going anywhere with you. Now please excuse me, my lord. I have work to do.'

Stuart took a room at The Bull and Bear and for a whole week tried to break down the iron barriers between himself and the girl he hungered for. Many times he spoke to her, but not once did she reply, walking away from him as if he didn't exist.

At the end of seven days, Melfort admitted his failure. It was clear that through his own folly he had lost Crystal and there was no point in staying and enduring the torture of being so close, yet so far away, from the woman without whom life would be nothing.

'I am leaving,' he said as they met on the stairs. 'I have done everything I can to make you see how much I love you. I shall never marry. I have no brother, so my name will die with me. A fitting punishment, no doubt, since my son is dead because of my neglect.'

Crystal watched him walk away, feeling hollow inside. In spite of her desperate desire for him, she had withstood him for a week, crying for him at night, hoping for a glimpse of him by day, but never letting him see that she was aware of him. Now he had gone for good and she felt the tears run down her cheeks as she picked up a pail and mop and went to clean the cellar floor.

Crystal managed to stay in Bristol for a further three weeks. Then she knew that she had to undo the harm she'd done to Stuart. Her words had been savage, designed to tear him apart, and he really didn't deserve that. Perhaps he might have given her the benefit of the doubt when they had met at that fateful ball, but his fury was understandable. It was also true that he knew nothing of her pregnancy and, if his mother was dying, it had been his duty to stay with her.

She counted out the money she had earned, sighing because it wasn't quite enough to pay the coach fare, even if she took a cheap seat on the roof. It would mean walking part of the way, but that couldn't be helped. She had to see Charlotte and ask her to tell the earl how sorry she was.

'What is it, luv?' Betsy Wheelwright had come in unheard, nodding as she saw the coins. 'Going after him, are you?'

'Him?'

Bessy laughed.

'Think I can't see what's under my nose. I saw the way he looked at you and you at him. Quarrelled again, did you?'

'He didn't quarrel with me, but I was awful to him.' Crystal found it hard to swallow. 'I've got to let him know I didn't mean all the things I said.'

'Well, why don't you go and see him? Lives in London, does he?'

'Yes, but I shan't go to him. You see, he's the son of a marquis and there can never be any future for us.'

'But the bairn was his?'

'Yes. He said it was his fault that Hamish died, but of course it wasn't.'

'Has he been looking for you for long?'

'He couldn't search for me himself because he was with his dying mother, but he paid many men to try to find me. I know that's true, because someone who once came to the shop told me so.'

'If you're not going to call on him, what are you going to do?'

'I shall ask a friend of his, whom I know, to pass on my regrets.'

'But you need a bit more to get there, is that it?'

'I can walk part of the way.'

'In your condition! Girl, you'd collapse before you'd gone half a mile. You've had enough good victuals put before you, but you haven't been eating them, have you?'

'I wasn't hungry. The food was excellent, but –'

'I know, I know. Here, take this and be on your way. And don't be too proud to see him if that's what he wants.'

'He won't want to see me again, not ever. I wouldn't expect him to after the way I treated him. And I can't take your money.'

''Course you can. Now, you go and get your things

together and I'll pack up some food for you, and this time
you eat it, mind.'

'You've been so kind.' Crystal caught one of Betsy's
workworn hands and held it against her cheek. 'I don't
know what I'd have done if you hadn't been here, especially
when Hamish died.'

'There, there, don't fret. The poor lamb's at peace now.
Come on, you're got no time for grizzling. You've got things
to put right.'

Crystal raised her head.

'Yes, I have, haven't I? Oh, Mrs Wheelwright, I do hope
he believes me when my apologies reach him. I think I shall
die, too, if he doesn't.'

Charlotte Somerset took one look at Crystal and put her
hands over her face.

'Lady Charlotte! What is it? I'm sorry if I'm intruding.
Shall I go?'

Charlotte's hands fell to her lap as she forced herself to
look at Crystal's shabby attire and wan face.

'Dear God,' she said at last. 'We did this to you. Crystal,
sit down, I beg you. We have much to talk about. Stuart
was right.'

Emerald eyes met violet ones.

'What did the earl say, my lady?'

'For pity's sake don't call me that. Haven't we got past
that stage, you and I? Those close to me call me Charlie,
although I don't suppose you feel much warmth towards
me after what has happened. As to what Melfort said – well
– he said you were ill and obviously you are. He is dying
inside because he thinks it is his fault.'

'But it isn't.'

'No, indeed. The blame lies with Rupert and me.'

'You didn't know in the beginning that I'd been forced to

take part in the masquerade, Lady Charlotte, did you? It was only when I told you the full facts later that you understood what had happened.'

'That's true, but it doesn't excuse my thoughtlessness. I should have stopped to think how upsetting such an experience would be to you, even if you'd wanted to join in our stupid plot.'

'It excuses it as far as I'm concerned.' For the first time Crystal relaxed, giving her companion a small smile. 'You were always very kind to me and I'll never forget it.'

'That's more than I deserve, but I'm so glad that you've come back to see Stuart. I've been afraid of what would happen to him – what he might do.'

'But I'm not going to see the earl.'

Charlotte gasped.

'Not going to see him? But you must put him out of his misery. If you didn't want to meet him, why did you come back to London?'

'Because I'm so ashamed of the terrible things I said to him when he was in Bristol. I even used his dead mother to hit out at him, I was furious with him, you see, for judging me as he did.'

'Yes, he was wrong, I agree, but you can't leave matters as they are.'

'That's why I've come to you. When you see the earl again, will you tell him how sorry I am and ask him to forgive me?'

'He's not in town at present. He left yesterday for Leddington Hall – that's in Wiltshire.'

'But he'll come back and you'll see him then.'

'Perhaps he'll return, perhaps he won't.' Charlotte's face crumpled in grief. 'What a dreadful injury I've inflicted on you both.'

'Not you.'

'I helped and Rupert, well, the less said about him the
better. He's been very strange of late. He swears that someone is following him about. A tall man, with dark curling
hair and bright blue eyes. He's getting to be afraid of his own
shadow. Perhaps he's going out of his mind; it would be a
fitting retribution.'

'Dark hair, blue eyes?' Crystal felt a spurt of alarm. 'Is he
sure?'

'He seems to be, but don't worry about him. Your baby;
you lost him. What can I say which will be of the slightest
comfort to you? Can you bear to talk about him?'

Crystal saw Charlotte's deep compassion and nodded.

'Yes, I think I can to you, Lady Ch – Charlie.'

'Thank you for that. Tell me about him. Stuart said that
you'd called him Hamish.'

'Yes, I'm not sure why. I just liked the name.'

'It's Melfort's second Christian name.'

For a moment Crystal's lips weren't steady.

'I didn't know that. Well, Hamish was very small and
feeble. I tried to pretend it wasn't so, but I think I knew after
the first twenty-four hours that I was going to lose him.'

'How agonizing for you. I don't think I could have borne
it.'

'One hasn't much choice. The inn-keeper's wife, Mrs
Wheelwright, was very kind to me. I'll never be able to repay
her for what she did. She even gave me some money so that I
could take the coach to its terminus. I was going to walk part
of the way.'

Charlotte's eyes filled with tears.

'An inn-keeper's wife. It was we who should have been
helping you. Melfort told me he'd have given his soul to have
seen his son.'

'He cared that much?' Crystal's question was almost a
prayer. 'Truly?'

'Yes, his son meant more to him than you will ever know.'

They talked for a while, two women sharing sorrow and renewing a friendship, Charlotte's sadness lifting for a while as she spoke of John and her love for him.

'I must go,' said Crystal regretfully when nearly an hour had passed. 'I have taken up enough of your time as it is. Please, Charlie, tell the earl how sorry I am.'

'No, I won't.'

Crystal gave her hostess a quick look and found her smiling.

'You tell him yourself. You know where to find him.'

'But how can I get there? I've no money, unless Mr Corry will lend me some. And I'm so shabby.'

'You've plenty of money.' Charlotte rose and took a box from a drawer in her tallboy. 'Here's the money you won that night at Reeve's – wasn't that the name of the place? I made Rupert give me every penny of it.'

'But I can't –'

'Of course you can. It belongs to you. Since Rupert had shared your winnings amongst those at the table, he had to dig into his own pocket to make up what he'd given away. Dear Crystal, take it and go. Don't make Stuart suffer any more. He was a fool, not a rogue, and he loves you so much. Isn't it the same for you?'

Crystal looked at the purse in her hand, suddenly marvellously and ridiculously happy.

'It's the same for me. Oh, Charlie, Charlie, yes! It's exactly the same for me.'

When Corry first saw Crystal he said nothing, just holding her close as they mourned for Fanny.

'I'm sorry about the baby,' he said at least. 'So very sorry.'

Crystal drew back, but kept Basil's hands in hers.

'How did you know that Hamish had died?'

'I know a good many things which you failed to write and tell me about. Melfort came to see me after he returned from Bristol. His friend, whose men traced you, found out quite a lot about the miseries you've endured these last months. Why didn't you tell me you needed help?'

'I couldn't ask for any more from you. You'd already been far too generous.'

'What nonsense. If it weren't for your present mourning I should be really angry with you. You should have realised that you could turn to me for anything at any time.'

'I know, I'm sorry. I was too proud, I suppose, and it was that pride which killed Hamish.'

'I doubt that. He wasn't strong from the start, was he?'

'No, but I feel that I failed him somehow.'

'Of course you didn't. It was God's Will. Hard to understand, but one has to accept.'

After a tearful reunion with Winnie, Crystal and Basil sat down to tea.

'Mrs Moloney thinks she's feeding an army, as usual,' chuckled Basil as he helped himself to a piece of cake. 'Still, she's justified this time. You're as skinny as the day we found you in the area. Eat up, my dear, or you'll be in trouble with our Winnie. Well, what are you going to do now? Your home is always here waiting for you, you know that.'

Shyly, Crystal told him of her plans and Basil gave a deep, satisfied sigh.

'Some sense at last. Then I'll arrange for a carriage for tomorrow, while you go and buy some new clothes. Have you any money?'

'Masses of it.' Crystal laughed. 'I've got my winnings from that ghastly place. I told you about. Mr Corry.'

'Yes?'

Crystal's smile had faded.

'I can't get out of my mind something which Lady Charlotte spoke of. Has a tall young man with dark curly hair and very blue eyes been to see you recently?'

'There was such a – a gentleman.'

'Did you tell him who attacked Fanny?'

For the first time in her life Crystal saw stark hatred in Basil Corry's face. Then it was gone as quickly as it had come.

'Yes,' he said very softly, 'I told him. That was the very least I could do for you and Fanny.'

The next day was a hot one. The journey to Wiltshire seemed endless and Crystal was so nervous that she found herself pleating the skirt of her new dress of yellow sarcenet with trembling fingers.

Her first sight of Leddington Hall did nothing to lift her agitation. It was a vast mansion lying in acres of ground, a fitting residence for a wealthy nobleman and no place for her to be.

The liveried butler, Arthur Mattson, received her as if she were a beggar.

'Is his lordship expecting you – er – madam?'

'Miss Yorke, and no he isn't.'

'He may not be At Home.'

'On the other hand, he might be.'

'I suppose it's possible.'

For a second Crystal felt like turning and running back to the safety of the carriage. Then she took herself in hand. Survivors didn't bolt because of servants with too high an opinion of their own importance.

'Then I suggest you go and find out,' she said and swept past the indignant Mattson. 'First, shew me where I may wait.'

The drawing-room into which she was ushered was blue and gold. There were heavy silk curtains, a magnificent oriental carpet underfoot, priceless furniture and many portraits of Stuart's forebears on the walls. Tall windows opened on to a terrace and Crystal could see peacocks strutting about shewing off their glory. They reminded her of the pompous man who had admitted her and she even managed a smile at the thought. Beyond the proud birds there was a rolling sweep of well tended lawn, edged with flowers, and in the far distance high trees giving privacy.

Stuart had just returned from riding when a footman came hurrying up to him with the news of his visitor.

'Miss Yorke? Are you sure?'

'Certain, m'lord. Leastways, that's what Mr Mattson told me to tell you.'

The earl waited until the servant had gone, needing to marshal his thoughts and pluck up what courage he had left. He couldn't imagine why Crystal had come. She had made plain her opinion of him at their last meeting. Then, all at once, he realised it didn't matter why. She was there; only a few yards away from him and he began to run.

When Melfort came in from the garden, Crystal clenched her hands behind her. Even from that distance she could see the hope and sadness mingled in his eyes and wanted to hold out her arms to him. But first she had to be certain that she hadn't left it too late.

'Lady Charlotte told me where to find you,' she said hesitantly. 'I didn't want to come myself. I asked her to give you a message, but she refused.'

'Thank God for Charlie.' The earl was equally cautious. He had done so much harm to the girl he worshipped and he wasn't quite sure what she would do if he caught her in his arms and kissed her with all the pent-up passion in him. 'What was the message?'

'I don't know how to say this, my lord.' Crystal was steeling herself for the final parting from the man she adored. 'I was abominably rude to you when you came to The Bull and Bear. What I said about your mother was inexcusable and I had to apologise for any hurt I caused.'

'Is that all you came for?' Stuart walked over to her. She was still too fine-drawn, but to him her beauty shone brighter than ever. He had thought his life was over; now the blood in his veins was beginning to race again. 'Was there another reason for this visit?'

Crystal blushed. His closeness was almost more than she could endure. Her body cried out silently for his touch and she knew it always would, no matter how far apart they were.

'I suppose I wanted to see you once more to say good-bye.'

'Why good-bye?'

'Well, we can't go back, can we? No one can ever go back.'

'No, but we can go forward. My darling, don't you know how much I love you and what hell this last year has been for me? I've been as a dead man because you weren't with me. Crystal, I want you to be my wife.'

They were words which Crystal had often dreamed about, but never expected to hear. Such perfect endings did not happen in real life.

'There is nothing I would like more than to be your wife,' she said despondently, 'but your father wouldn't permit it.'

'He has already agreed. I wouldn't have cared if he hadn't, but he's been most obliging and has even given me a commission for you.'

'A commission?'

He smiled, one hand brushing the red curls away from her cheek.

'I'll tell you about that later. Now there is something more important I have to do.'

He took her in his arms, feeling her instant response, and thanking God for second chances.

'I'm sorry about our baby,' he said gently. 'We must do better next time.'

'We will.' Crystal needed Stuart's kiss and his lips were very close to hers, yet she had to have one last word of assurance that the happiness wouldn't be snatched away from her just as she succumbed to it. 'Are you sure, Stuart?'

'I'm quite sure.' His hold tightened, feeling her warmth against him. 'My very dearest girl; I shall never let you out of my sight again.'

When Matson opened the door to announce the arrival of the Marquis of Ravenmore, he found the earl and his pert visitor locked in an embrace so unashamedly sensual that his discreet cough was more like a choking fit.

There was a glint of mischief in Crystal's eyes as the earl released her and she turned to face the startled butler.

'You see there was no need to worry,' she said in some satisfaction, her hand tucked safely in Stuart's. 'The earl was At Home to me after all.'